DREAD
SOFTLY
A COLLECTION

CARYN LARRINAGA

Cover by Rooster Republic Press

Print ISBN: 978-0-9990200-7-4
Ebook ISBN: 978-0-9990200-6-7
Library of Congress Control Number: 2021908374

A Twisted Tree Press Publication
North Salt Lake City, UT
www.TwistedTreePress.com

PRAISE FOR DREAD SOFTLY

For Joe.

I can finally admit that your Goosebumps collection was better than mine.

Content warnings are listed at the back of the book.

TABLE OF CONTENTS

ACKNOWLEDGMENTS

Call me Captain Obvious, but I love horror. I sometimes feel like I shouldn't. It shouldn't make sense for someone with this much anxiety to seek out stories about nightmare scenarios and terrifying creatures. But for some reason, watching someone navigate an exorcism or unravel a vengeful ghost's secrets is a great antidote to my real-life worries.

I think it started with my dad. In fact, it might date all the way back to a night in the late '80s when he rented *House* and *The Gate* to watch with my older brother and me. He probably thought that, as they were horror comedies, I wouldn't be so scared. (Flash forward to thirty-plus years later and I still don't trust bathroom vanities with mirrored doors or the jagged pits uprooted trees leave behind.) But despite the uptick in my nightmares, I was also instantly addicted to that feeling. I couldn't resist seeking it out again, the same way I can't resist eating way too many fancy pastries even though I know I'll be paying a horrible price for it within a few hours.

My mom picked up the baton once the horror bug burrowed its way into my brain. She helped me find books to feed the addiction, like the ever-classic *Scary Stories to Tell in the Dark* by

Alvin Schwartz, *Great Ghosts* by Daniel Cohen, *Wait Till Helen Comes* by Mary Downing Hahn, the Scary Stories for Sleep-overs series, stacks of Goosebumps by R.L. Stine, *Bruce Coville's Book of Ghosts*, the Point Horror series (especially *Funhouse* by Diane Hoh), and so many others. I read them over and over. Ghosts, monsters, haunted objects, zombie children—I couldn't get enough.

Being a spooky little girl didn't come with many perks, but arguably the best one was developing an invisible magnetic field that drew me to other weirdos. Exhibit A: Joe Fisher, with whom I spent my elementary years trading paperbacks, crafting mocktails with rad names like "Avenged Murders," and trying to figure out what the hell was going on in *Altered States*.

My horror circle soon expanded to include Jill Johnson, who introduced me to the world of Vincent Price and has always been down to rent random videos (the more absurd the premise, the better). Weekends in junior high meant raw cookie dough, Fun Dip, and scary movies. As adults, we revisit that magical formula as often as we can (but we bake the cookies before eating them now).

In college, I met my all-time favorite horror-binge buddy and married his pants off. Horror is always the number-one genre in our house, best enjoyed with a bowl of slightly over-salted popcorn, a cat on my lap, and Kelly Burt by my side. He listens to each of my stories, often more than once, and helps me push through the blocks to say exactly what I'm trying to say.

When I line up so many incredible, loving, supportive people like this, it actually doesn't feel weird at all that I love horror. I love it because of them, because I associate it with some of my favorite people on the planet.

How could I *not* love it?

I have to thank C.R. Langille, organizer for the Utah chapter of the Horror Writers Association, for helping me along the path from horror fan to horror creator. The UHWA's open call for their annual horror anthology inspired me to write short horror with an eye toward publication, and I've since tricked C.R. into being my critique partner as often as I can. He helped me with many of the stories in this collection, and they shine more brightly because of his thoughtful insights and pitch-perfect suggestions. I'm so grateful for his generosity.

I'd also like to thank the publishers who gave these stories their first homes, including The NoSleep Podcast, Post-to-Print Publishing, Nocturnal Sirens Publishing, the UHWA, the League of Utah Writers, Infinite Press, and the Salt City Genre Writers.

Huge thanks to my incomparable editor, Jennie Stevens, for helping me take a jumbled collection of stories originally published in different places and giving them a cohesive style. Thanks also to my proofreader, Beverly Bernard, who stood as the final guard between this book and your hands.

Last but never least, thank you for reading my stories. It means so much to me. Maybe it's cheesy to say, but you're the reason my author dreams came true.

And with that, I'll leave you with some of my favorite nightmares. ♥

DREAD
SOFTLY

NO SOLICITING

At twelve o'clock in the afternoon, just as it had every day for the last five weeks, the bell rang. Doris scowled at the front door from her indentation on the sagging couch and braced herself for the subsequent rings.

"Go away! Go away!" Frankie shouted from his perch.

"Frankie, quiet!" Doris hissed.

Her admonition made no difference. The parrot hadn't listened to her in twenty-five years; why on earth would he start now? And no matter how much either the bird or the woman told the salesman to leave them alone, he paid her even less heed than Frankie.

The doorbell rang again.

"Ma'am?" The salesman's voice pierced through the reinforced door. "I know you're in there. Please, I'd just like to talk to you for a few minutes about your home's security."

Doris rolled her eyes and turned her TV's volume up as far as she could stand it. She had never stood on her front porch while the TV was on—or ever, come to think of it—but she felt confident the salesman could hear the soap opera stars shouting about the main character's sister returning from the dead. Doris grinned, imagining the salesman getting sucked into the story but never having the satisfaction of knowing how it ended. She would turn the volume down before any kind of big reveal. It would be easy; she could always feel them coming, the way the mood of the music would shift and intensify right before the surprise came.

The faint sound of a fist pounding on the door reached her ears through the noise from the television set. The doorbell rang a third time. A minute later, the top of a blue baseball cap bobbed past the front window, away from the porch.

Joints creaking, Doris struggled off the couch and shambled to the window. The salesman, a youngster somewhere in his early twenties, stopped at the end of her long driveway and looked back at the house. She didn't hide herself. He knew she was home. He knew that she knew that he knew, but it didn't stop him from harassing her day after day. Had she been so headstrong in her youth? The twin veils of time and malnutrition obscured her memory. A hundred years was far too many to reflect upon with such an empty stomach.

"Go away!" the parrot shrieked.

Doris snorted and turned away from the window. "Stupid bird. He's gone. For today, anyway."

Not bothering to turn down the television, she shuffled into the kitchen. A frying pan with a thin layer of oil waited on the gas stove. She retrieved her last packet of meat from the old, grumbling freezer and threw the steak into the pan. As the thigh sizzled and hissed, a jagged grin spread over her wrinkled face. Her freezer was empty. The next delivery would come tonight—fresher meat, and the extra little something she had ordered. Soon, she would have peace again.

TOO EXCITED TO SLEEP, Doris perched on a short wooden stool by the back door, watching as the second hand of the big clock over the stove ticked closer to midnight. The hour came, and she craned her neck, straining to hear the telltale sounds of her monthly delivery.

There would be no knock, no doorbell ring. The faceless, nameless courier never deviated from the routine. Every thirty days, he left sixty cutlets of fresh meat and any other requested sundries—pellets and produce for Frankie, poison for the rats in the basement, cooking oil—in the old wooden box on the back porch. Doris would confirm the delivery with a phone call, usually the next morning, and the money would get transferred from her account to the company's.

In over two decades of solitude, Doris had only needed to change this service once. A few years into their contract, the first company had gotten lazy, started cutting corners with the harvest. She had felt the age of the meat at once; her joints had locked up, and she lost several teeth. It had taken all her energy to telephone the remaining brethren in her little book of contacts—even then, too many names had been crossed out—but luckily, one other of her kind smart enough to close themselves off from the world had recommended an alternate service.

The new company proved to be excellent. They sourced the meat only from the most reputable morgues and guaranteed harvest and flash freezing within forty-eight hours of death. They were discreet and diligently protected the privacy of their customers.

Best of all, delivery was never late.

A low thump sounded from the porch. Doris's black eyes lit up with excitement. It took all her willpower to wait a full five minutes, a window of time required by the delivery company for their staff's safety. At last, she unfastened the chain, released the four dead bolts, and opened the door. With as much speed as she could manage, she ferried the packets of meat from the delivery box into her kitchen. Beneath the last paper-wrapped package, she found the thing she had been anticipating as much as—more than, really—the meat: a small magnetic sign.

After relocking the back door, she carried the sign through the house to the front entryway. It took several long minutes to get the steel slab open. Unlike the locks at the back of the house, these hadn't been turned in too many years to count.

At last, the door opened, and Doris slapped the new sign on the front with a triumphant, "Ha!"

Silver letters spelling NO SOLICITING gleamed in the moonlight.

"Let him try to come now," she told Frankie.

The bird, asleep in his cage beneath a white sheet, didn't answer. It was for the best. She wouldn't have liked what he had to say.

DORIS BROKE her fast early the next day, heating the oil on her stove well before the normal hour. Wielding her butcher's knife with more energy than usual, she cut the steak into thin strips and tossed them into the pan. The aroma wafting upward told her this meat had come from someone who'd been alive less than two days before. It was markedly more fresh than what she'd been eating the past week, and she felt its effects mere minutes after finishing her meal. The inflammation in her joints subsided, the skin on her hands smoothed out, and her mind sharpened. She stood in front of the mirror by the front door for a while, admiring the difference in her face.

She didn't look a day over eighty.

"Hey, old lady!" Frankie squawked from his cage.

"Oh, shut up." She touched the corners of her eyes, where deep crow's feet betrayed too many decades of glaring at the bird. She wondered what she would've looked like at sixty, fifty, or even thirty-five. With enough fresh meat, could she see?

It would have to be quite fresh, her sister's voice purred inside her mind. *Not even dead a minute, and raw, so very raw—*

"Quiet!" Doris shouted. She glared at her reflection, seeing far too many of her sister's features in the face that glared back. But wrinkles had never softened Ethel's face; her skin had been smooth as glass when she went mad.

From the box above her head, the doorbell chimed. Doris jumped, staring at the door with wide eyes.

"Ma'am?" the salesman's voice called. He knocked a few times, then rang the bell again. "Hello? We're having a sale on motion sensors and cameras. You can't put a price on your safety!"

Doris glanced at Frankie, her mouth open in hopeless shock. The salesman stood on the porch, inches away from her NO SOLICITING sign, ringing her doorbell with impunity. She backed away from the door, grateful for her fresh breakfast as she crouched on the floor beside the bird's cage, something her knees wouldn't have let her do the day before.

"What do I do?" she whispered.

"Eat him! Eat him!" Frankie suggested.

Doris smacked the bird's cage. "Don't be absurd."

"Eat him!" the bird urged again.

"You'd like that, wouldn't you?" Doris said. "You'd love to see me go insane, leave this house on a binge like your old master."

Frankie bobbed his gray head in his cage.

"What, you think someone will come rescue you? Take over your care and feeding when I'm gone, like I did after Ethel? There's nobody left who even knows we're here, you stupid creature."

The parrot held still a moment, head cocked to the side as though considering her words. Then he blinked his yellow eyes and screeched, "Old lady, old lady!"

Doris balled her hands into fists and shuddered. If any meat aside from human flesh offered her any sustenance at all, she would eat the damn bird and be done with it.

"I should leave you on the porch," she told him. "Cage and all. Let this foolish salesman take you home."

As though in answer to his title, the nuisance outside rang the bell again. After a moment, he beat on the door, pounding against the metal.

Doris shook with rage. From the height of the sound, he had to be banging his knuckles right on top of the sign she had stuck there the night before. There was no question; he saw the words, but they did nothing to deter him.

Each knock reverberated in her bones. Her teeth rattled, and she dragged her nails from her shoulders to her elbows. "Go away!" she screamed at the door. "Leave me alone!"

"Sounds like this is a bad time," the young man called. "I'll come back another day."

At that, anger took over Doris's body. She leaped to her feet, and her hand closed around the top dead bolt.

"Open!" Frankie screeched from his cage. "Open, open!"

His voice snapped Doris back to her senses. Her fingers fell away from the bolt, and she ran a shaking hand down her face.

That had been far too close. In her mind's eye, she saw what had almost happened: flinging open the door and falling upon the man, ripping and tearing at his throat with her teeth like the ancient, savage monsters from whom her kind had descended. She remembered the feel of hot blood in her throat and gulped. Once, and only once, had she given in to the wild desires that lay deep within her belly. At Ethel's urging, she had tasted the flesh of a man whose heart still beat in his chest. The memory of the sudden surge of strength and the sharpening of her mind gave Doris a fraction of the high she'd experienced that day, and she sagged against the cool metal door, heart racing and cheeks flushed.

You can feel it again, Ethel promised inside her mind. *It would be so easy.*

"No!" Doris shook her head and hugged her knees against her chest. She couldn't follow Ethel down that dark path, no matter how her sister's voice called to her. She had seen firsthand what happened when someone gave in to their bloodlust. The line between eternal youth and certain madness was thinner than

Doris's ragged hair.

When her breathing slowed, she pulled herself to her feet and hobbled to the stove. Another few days of solid, unfrozen meals and her sister's voice would retreat to the corners of her mind. The fuller she was, the safer everyone would be.

DORIS WOKE to the sound of rain pounding on the roof, and a deep sigh escaped her lungs. Foul weather was a far more effective deterrent than a flimsy little sign. At last, a day of peace. She lay in bed awhile, planning her morning. First, she would have a fresh steak from the refrigerator, one of the last before she would need to switch to the frozen ones. Then she would spend the day cleaning and straightening up the house while the boost of energy lasted.

She padded into the kitchen to fry up her breakfast. In front of the fridge, the floor glinted strangely in the gray light from the window. She reached down, testing the sheen with a finger.

"Water," she murmured, furrowing her brow and glancing at the sink. The faucet was still, and she heard no signs of dripping. Where else could it have come from?

She whipped her head toward the refrigerator, registering the silence around her. The entire house was eerily quiet. Thunder cracked overhead as she flicked the light switch on and off to no effect.

The power was out.

Doris swore, and Frankie picked up the word, repeating it at top volume in the living room.

"Quiet!" she shouted.

"Quiet! Quiet!" Frankie screeched, hopping in his cage.

Ignoring the bird, she tore open the freezer's door. Half the frost inside had melted and pooled on the kitchen floor. The rest had soaked into the paper-wrapped packages she'd thrown into the compartment just two days before. She touched one; it was no longer frozen, but it smelled far from fresh. Bad or even diseased flesh wouldn't kill her, but old meat would do nothing to keep her body from racing toward its true age.

The real tragedy waited in the refrigerator. The antique appliance struggled to keep cool even with a running motor, and an unknown number of hours with no power had allowed every gasp of cold air to escape through the cracks in the door's seal. The freshest steaks, the ones she'd been counting on to wind her body's clock back to seventy or so, had turned.

She wasted no time grabbing the telephone and dialing the delivery company. "The power's gone out," she barked into the receiver when they answered. "Half my food is ruined. I need a replacement delivery."

"No problem at all," the young man on the phone replied. "We'll have that to you by midnight."

The arrangements made, Doris fired up the gas stove, grateful she at least didn't need to eat her breakfast raw.

BOTH THE RAIN and the power outage continued through the next morning, but the delivery box on the back porch was empty when Doris checked it.

"We're currently experiencing a high call volume," a recorded voice explained when she called the delivery company. "Please continue to hold."

Swearing, Doris hung up the phone and checked the freezer. The situation was even worse than the day before, and she retrieved a soggy packet of meat with a disgusted groan.

Her joints ached as she prepared her breakfast at a fraction of her usual pace, not bothering to cut up the steak before searing it. She winced each time she glimpsed her hands as she ate; the blue veins beneath her paper-thin skin had never been so visible before. She would look and feel her full 106 years by the day's end.

It seemed like a waste of energy to chew meat that was too old to do much more than give her the energy to chew more meat. Was this how humans felt about their food? Eating just for the sake of having enough calories to move their frail bodies around, knowing they would continue to age and weaken with every passing day?

How pointless.

But humans were lucky in some ways. She had watched the reality TV shows about the people who were as trapped in their houses as she was in hers. At least they had visitors, family and friends who could help them pass the time. There were a handful of other unnatural beings left in her book of contacts, but none of them were any more likely to leave their hiding places than she was to leave hers and couldn't be counted on to keep her company. And no matter how much a human ate, they would never go mad and lose the ability to stop killing and eating before turning on their own kind.

I would never have hurt you, Ethel claimed inside her mind. *I only wanted to help you be free.*

Doris snorted and shook her head. That was another way these humans on the television were luckier than her; their siblings would never have to kill them just to stop their bloodlust from exposing their way of life.

Well, at least I died young, Ethel's voice sneered. *I don't even recognize you, old woman.*

"Old woman! Old woman!" Frankie echoed from his perch.

Doris lacked the strength to argue with either of them. She sank down onto the couch and reached for the remote before remembering there was no power. Too tired to get up, she closed her eyes and tried to nap.

DING-DONG!

The ring of the doorbell startled Doris, and she jerked forward.

"Ding-dong! Ding-dong!" Frankie helpfully sang.

Doris struggled to her feet, wondering why on earth the delivery

man would ring the bell. Twelve hours late, in broad daylight…
and at her front door. She was halfway across the room before she
realized he would never do such a thing. And that meant it had to
be—

"Ma'am?" the salesman called through the door. "Are you
home? I'd love to come in and chat with you about your home
security. Do you currently have an alarm provider?"

Before she could stop them, Doris's feet carried her across the
floor and into the foyer. Her hands were upon the lock, ready to pull
the door open.

Yes, Ethel encouraged. *Let him come in. He's been begging for
this for weeks.*

Doris examined herself in the mirror beside the door. New
wrinkles lined her face, but it was Ethel's dark eyes that stared
back at her.

"I couldn't," Doris told her reflection.

But you want to, Ethel said. *I can feel it. You've wanted this for
twenty-five long years. Eat him. Drink his blood while it still pumps
through him, and you'll be young again within the hour.*

The salesman pounded on the door. Doris rested her hand
on it, inches from where his fist connected with the thick steel,
and she eyed her skin with distaste. Her stomach growled. She
glanced helplessly at her reflection, and Ethel's eyes repeated their
argument.

A memory flooded into Doris's mind. She remembered the day,
so many years ago, when Ethel first convinced her to break the
boundary between fresh meat and living flesh. The taste of warm
blood coated her throat, and she licked her lips as her fingertips
found their way to the topmost dead bolt yet again.

The door groaned as she inched it open.

"Need a hand?" the salesman asked.

"Yes, please," she said, stepping back. "It's an old door.
Stubborn, like me."

The salesman laughed as he pushed his way inside the house. As Doris had guessed, he was in his early twenties, fresh-faced and tanned from day after day canvassing suburban neighborhoods. His blue cap matched his collared polo shirt, and his backpack lent an extra layer of innocence to his already youthful appearance. It had been so many years since she'd been this close to a living human. He smelled as fresh as the rain outside.

Delicious, Ethel's voice said in chorus with her own thoughts.

He wiped his feet on the seldom-used mat inside the door, shrugging an apology for dripping water onto the hardwood.

Doris shook her head. "Please don't worry about it. Come in. Sit down."

As the salesman walked past his cage, Frankie screeched, "Get out! Get out!"

The young man nodded to the bird. "Is it friendly?"

Frankie bobbed on his perch. "Frankie, be my friend! My friend!"

"When he wants to be," she said. "I would keep your fingers away from the bars. He'll nip at you, and his little beak might break your skin."

The man who'd been pestering Doris for weeks slung his backpack off his shoulders and sank into Doris's spot on the couch. He took off his baseball cap, ran a hand through his thick hair, and nodded at her cluttered living room. "Lovely home. How long have you been here?"

"Oh, about twenty-five years." She smiled at him, wondering if her hair would grow back as thick and dark as his after she ate his scalp. "Tea?"

"Yes, please."

He opened his backpack and began pulling out pamphlets and pricing sheets, and she left him in the bird's company. She rounded the corner into her kitchen and pulled down the teapot as quickly as she could manage, marveling at the speed of her hands as she reached for the box of rat poison she kept in the cupboard. She moved faster than she had just an hour ago, bolstered by the anticipation of her first truly good meal since the day she killed Ethel.

The memory of stabbing her sister with a silver knife stopped Doris's hands just before they closed around the poison. She had ended Ethel's life... but why? What could make her do such a thing? Her mind clouded. Ethel's voice tried to drown out the truth. But after a moment, Doris remembered.

Ethel had given in to the bloodlust. She hadn't been able to stop. And even in an era of serial killers and highway murderers, the humans had become suspicious.

I was weak, Ethel explained. *You've always been the strong one. You stopped after just one taste of a fresh kill. How many of our kind can say the same?*

It was true. Not many had the will to secrete themselves away, to allow their bodies to grow old and keep a distance from their prey. Once they gave in to their darkest desires, the lucky ones were put down by other members of their flock. The rest got sloppy enough to attract the attention of cleverer-than-average humans, and some hunter stepped in to stop their rampage. Too few had the willpower to stop killing once they started, to cease bingeing once that first juicy morsel passed their lips.

Doris eyed the butcher's knife in the block beside the stove. Yes, that was the compromise. She would allow herself just a taste of living flesh. A few mouthfuls, nothing more. Enough to turn back the clock a few decades, feel closer to her normal self. Then she would stop, carve up the rest of his body, and store it the way her mother had taught her when she was a child. In the decade of plenty the humans called the Dust Bowl, her mother had dried meat into jerky, striking a perfect balance between freshness and safety. Decayed enough to keep the madness at bay, new enough to keep their family young and healthy. No freezer required.

"Sugar?" she called to the young man in her living room as she poured the poison into his cup.

"No, thank you."

With shaking hands, she carried the pair of teacups into the living room. The salesman accepted his doctored tea, smelling it with a smile before resting it on the coffee table. Doris sat down on the opposite end of the couch, her unpoisoned cup still in her hands.

"Not safe!" Frankie screeched. "Get out!"

Doris glared at the bird.

"Quite a vocabulary he has," the salesman said.

"Television," she explained. "He watches it with me, and I watch it a lot."

The young man laughed. "You and me both. Have you seen our commercials? They run pretty often."

"I haven't. You must be freezing after walking around in all this rain." She sipped her tea and nodded toward his cup. "Go on, drink up while it's hot."

Ignoring the tea, the salesman handed her a pricing sheet with text and numbers in large print. She raised a hairless eyebrow, at once grateful and irritated. Soon, she would have her full eyesight back and wouldn't need thoughtfully oversized literature.

"Have you ever had a home security system before?" he asked.

Doris shook her head. "Never needed one."

"Could've fooled with me that big steel door." The young man grinned. "I haven't seen one of those outside a bank before. But the trick is to combine that with the newer technology we have available, like doorbell cameras and motion sensors. Times are changing. It's not safe to leave your door unlocked anymore. You never know who might turn up on your porch."

Doris wanted to laugh. Once she had her strength back, no human could defend against her if she wanted to come into their home and eat them while they slept. No camera could stop her teeth from ripping into their tender flesh—

"Not safe!" Frankie screeched again. "Run away!"

"Quiet!" Doris shouted. Then she smiled an apology at the salesman. "I've got to stop letting him watch those late-night horror movies after I've gone to bed. He's picking up the strangest phrases."

The salesman laughed and picked up his teacup. "They're funny little creatures, aren't they? I've always kind of wanted one."

Doris snorted. "He's all yours."

"Mmm." The salesman sniffed his tea. "Smells wonderful."

He raised the cup to his lips, staring down at the liquid that would soon render him immobile. Doris wiped her mouth, which threatened to overflow with a sudden abundance of saliva.

"Look out!" Frankie screeched.

As the cup touched his lips, the salesman flicked his eyes upward. His gaze met Doris's. Any trace of friendliness had disappeared, and she recognized the sudden hardness that took its place. It was the same glint of sharpened instinct that had filled Ethel's eyes at the end—the piercing stare of a killer.

Run! Ethel's voice screamed in her mind.

But it was too late. The hunter was upon her in an instant. She had no energy to fend off his attack and moved too slowly to stop the descent of the blade in his hand. She screamed as it stabbed her, writhing in agony as the silver burned into her flesh.

"Bye-bye!" Frankie said.

"Damn bird," she muttered. Then she lay still.

The hunter rose, cleaning his knife on the edge of his blue shirt. The kill had been quick and clean, the way his father taught him. He left her valuables in place, picking up only the little leather-bound book of contacts Doris kept by the phone. He flipped through the pages, smiling at the handful names that hadn't been crossed out yet and recognizing some of the ones that had. Pocketing the book, he strode across the living room and picked up Frankie's cage.

"Come on, buddy," he told the bird. "You're mine now."
Frankie bobbed on his perch. He didn't mind at all.

EMPIRE OF DIRT

"Don't take this the wrong way," Drake tells me, "but I wish you hadn't come."

"I thought you wanted me to make peace with Hannah," I say.

"Yeah, but not like this. Not by crashing her birthday party."

I frown at him. "It should have been *our* birthday party."

"I know. And I wish it was." He glances across the cavernous kitchen toward my twin sister, who is currently engaged in the family tradition of knocking down one shot for every seven years you've been alive. A crowd of cousins cheer as Hannah slams her fifth shot glass down onto the countertop. The older relatives, the ones who've passed the seven-shot mark and retired from the game, watch the proceedings with scorn as though they weren't booting and rallying in their younger days. "But if my dad sees you, he'll throw you out on your ass."

I'm not worried about my uncle. He's the kind of guy who likes to puff out his chest and make a scene, but it's been over two decades since he stopped doing birthday shots. I'd like to see the old fart try to give me the bum's rush.

Not that my illness has left me in much better shape. Last week I couldn't grip a spoon, let alone fend off angry relatives. Yesterday

I could hardly stand, but today I'm feeling better. Good enough to do what needs to be done.

Good enough to have no regrets for last night's actions at the lab.

I scratch the inside of my left arm absently, searching for the injection marks at my elbow through my sweatshirt and wincing when my fingertips find them. Wielding a hypodermic needle takes more dexterity than I had yesterday, but I couldn't trust anyone to help me without ratting me out to the compliance team, which is outrageous. It's my company. My product. I should be able to do whatever the hell I want with it.

And what a product it is. I flex my fingers, testing myself, and a grin spreads over my face. Unless I'm imagining it—which I admit is possible, given the projected side effects of this new cocktail—I'm as stable as I was before the myopathy took hold. The drug reversed twelve months of decline in less than twelve hours. Incredible! Once it gets approved, it'll make my company a household name.

Of course, we still need to wait for the human trials to begin. It's a long road, but as long as I can keep dosing myself, I might live to see the finish line.

"Hey, are you okay?" Drake asks. "You look… weird."

"I'm fine." I raise my head to show him my smile. "Just nervous."

He nods, but doubt lingers in his eyes. Doubt and hope and—yep, there it is—the little flash of greed I see every time we get together. It's small, but he and I both know it's the reason he still reaches out to me. Unlike the rest of my family, he's shrewd enough to think being nice to me might earn him a place in my will.

And he's right. Well, he used to be. Getting sick puts things into perspective, changes our plans.

Shit, it flat-out changes who we are.

WHEN WE WERE KIDS, our parents joked that I was Hannah's echo. Born second, I was never as loud as her. Never as bold. For a long time, I was more comfortable allowing her to take the lead while I drafted behind her, out of the spotlight. It was easier.

Hannah didn't have to work to make things easier on herself. Somehow, when our zygote split, all the wit, charm, looks, and luck got sucked straight into her half. The attention lavished on her by our teachers and parents fattened her ego the way errant matter fattens a black hole, and the older we got, the stronger her pull became. At our eighteenth birthday party, her name took up a full three-quarters of the cake, barely leaving room at the bottom for an awkward "Tabatha" in suspiciously discolored frosting.

"Make a wish, Hannah!" our mother prompted, holding a FunSaver up to her eye.

We leaned toward the candles together. The flickering lights played across Hannah's features, but I felt only shadows on my face. As I stared at my name—crammed onto the cake as an obvious afterthought—the words that popped into my head surprised me.

I wish they loved me as much as they love Hannah.

Beside me, my twin whispered her wish to the candles, so low only I could hear it. "I don't want to share a dorm room with Tabatha."

My wish didn't come true. Until their dying day, my parents favored Hannah over me to an immeasurable degree, even after I got sick freshman year, moved home, and transferred to the community college.

"At least until we figure out what's going on with you," my mother promised. "But all these diagnostic tests…. Well, they're expensive, sweetie. We need to save money somewhere."

As always, Hannah got everything she wanted. She got her

performing arts degree at NYU, echo-free.

F<small>ROM MY HIDING</small> place behind my grandmother's hanging spider plant, I watch my sister, marveling at the stark differences between us. She hasn't changed in the years since we last spoke; she's still gorgeous with toned muscles and rosy cheeks that glow with health. She laughs at something and claps our cousin Braden on the back, and the sound of the slap carries across the hubbub of voices that bounce off the tiled walls.

And here I am, excited that I can squeeze my fingers into a fist again. She has everything that matters, and soon, she'll get what she deserves.

Not yet, though. I have a moment in mind to reveal myself. Until then, Hannah won't see me coming. Nobody will. Apart from Drake, none of my relatives have recognized me. On top of the fact that I've lost forty pounds, I dyed my hair black to cover up how brittle and straw-like my light brown strands have gotten. I'm wearing my oldest and most worn gym clothes instead of the designer sheath dresses I used to strut around in. I even swapped out my thick plastic frames for a pair of double-bridge wire rims that look like something my father would have owned.

My style is a far cry from the way I looked last time I was on the cover of *Forbes*, and I've been off social media since the weight loss started, so nobody but Drake knows what the disease has done to me. If I survive this thing, I don't want some website reminding me in a year or two of how shitty I look right now. Hey, Tabatha, remember when you weighed the same as a middle school cheerleader? Gee, thanks, Facebook.

I'm not the only one who's changed. It's been a long time since I've seen my relatives, and they've aged in the last decade. Drake's dad, Henry, is a wisp of a man now, and my grandmother has shrunk so much that her little white-haired head doesn't even reach the top of her high-backed dining chair.

My fist tightens. They're all here celebrating Hannah. How many of them remembered me today? And if they did, how many thought of me with kindness? Probably none. If I entered their minds at all, it was to curse me for supposedly screwing my sister out of her half of "our" business. Like she wasn't the one who left me behind.

Is it too late to change things? I'm strong again. Healthy. If I leave right now, I can undo what I've done, and Hannah will never know what I almost gave her for our birthday.

A bitter laugh escapes my dry throat. It catches on my raw esophagus, triggering a coughing fit that gives way to a gagging, extended exhale.

Drake's eyes widen in alarm as I try to suck in a breath. "Are you sure you're okay?"

I nod and open my mouth to tell him I'm fine, but my nerves—and a sudden bout of nausea—send bile rushing up my throat. Not wanting to announce myself by puking all over Grandma's gold-flecked countertops, I shove past Drake and duck into the half bath off the kitchen.

Viscous yellow fluid erupts from my lips the instant my knees touch the bathroom floor. Happily, somebody has left the toilet seat up. I heave for a few minutes, gagging and panting, then stare into the bowl. My eyes unfocus as I search through my memory, trying to recall the list of potential side effects for the drug I injected myself with last night.

The preclinical team hasn't put a final report together yet, so all I have to go on are the scraps of information from their daily summaries. Pain at the injection site. Nausea. Dizziness. Euphoria.

"Four for four." I giggle. "Who's the lucky one now?"

OUR PARENTS' death hit Hannah hard. We were twenty-five, and she announced she felt "rudderless" for the first time in her life. I found it easier to throw myself into my work than to process the sudden end to my complicated relationship with my parents, but she stepped back from acting to grieve in our hometown. She spent most of her days mooning around my home office, watching me try to line up investors for my fledgling biotech company.

"Your voice is too meek," she told me one day after I failed—yet again—to secure a pitch meeting. "You've got to be more confident."

I rolled my eyes. "Right. Like it's that easy."

"It is. Watch." She snatched up my yellow legal pad. Her eyes sparkled as she scanned the contact information of the potential backers I'd found through weeks of painstaking research. She studied it for a few seconds, then dialed my phone. When a muffled voice on the other end of the line greeted her, she responded with my name. "Hi, Mr. Hathaway, this is Tabatha Thorn, returning your call.... That wasn't you? My apologies, my secretary must've written it down incorrectly. One moment." She covered the mouthpiece with her hand and shouted at an empty corner of the room. "Thomas, didn't you say Charles Hathaway called about rescheduling our pitch meeting? Oh, *Berkshire* Hathaway. Of course." She lowered her voice again, telling Mr. Hathaway, "There's been a mix-up. I'm so sorry to have wasted your—oh, you are? Well, we've nearly locked up the first round here, but let me see what I can work out...."

Fifteen minutes later, my first pitch meeting was on the books. Hannah hung up the phone and chuckled to herself.

"How was that?" she asked. "I play you better than you do, right?"

I stared at her. "How do you do that?"

She winked. "Magic."

"Come on, seriously."

"I mean it." She shrugged. "It's just…. I don't know. Confidence. Tell the universe what you want. Don't ask for it. Say it like it's already yours and take it."

A vision struck me then: Hannah as the face of the company, luring investors to our cause with her irresistible gravitational pull while I worked behind the scenes to find treatments for every ailment, starting with my own. No more phone calls or pitch meetings. Just research, development, and success.

"I wish you would come work with me," I said. "I know you've got acting and everything, but wouldn't it be fun? You and me against the world, like when we were kids."

"Really?" She folded her arms behind her head, exhaling as she considered me. "That was pretty fun. And—oh! Have you named your company yet?"

"I haven't filed the final paperwork, but I'm thinking Thorn Technologies."

She snorted. "Okay, now I have to get involved. Come on, you dork. The name is right there, and I'm not even the fancy science genius."

"Okay, cut the suspense. What is it?"

"Twin Helix."

The room brightened. The name was perfect. For the first time, the company felt real.

Hannah told me she would consider joining my team, but two days later her agent called with an offer to costar in a summer blockbuster. My sister bailed, but I took her advice to heart. With the magic of mind over matter, I imitated her imaginary, confident version of Tabatha Thorn in the pitch meeting and secured my first round of funding.

Her movie flopped, but Twin Helix R&D thrived. I soon had to leave the lab behind to run the company, but every day, I channeled Confident Tabatha and told the universe what I wanted. Funding. A good research team. And more than anything else, a way to rid myself of this disease.

Hannah called a year after we launched and asked my secretary to tell me she wanted back in. I never called her back.

Until now, I didn't see the point.

THE BABBLE of voices on the other side of the bathroom door quiets. If that means what I think it means, it's nearly time—either to do what I came here to do or sneak out while everyone's distracted by the promise of cake. I pull myself to my feet and push my sleeves up to my elbows so I can wash my hands in the sink. As the water heats up, I examine my reflection. If I stay, will they even recognize me?

They will when I start talking. My voice is the only thing about me that hasn't changed.

In the harsh light that surrounds the bathroom mirror, the bruises at the crook of my elbow look angry and purple. A fresh wave of nausea rocks me, and I lurch forward, catching my thigh on the sink. A crack sounds from the pocket of my sweatpants. When I retrieve my cell phone, its glass face is spider-webbed with damage.

"Shit."

As though complaining about being injured, my phone pings. An email message appears on the broken screen.

URGENT—POSTPONE PHASE ONE CLINICAL TRIAL. SEVERE MUTATIONS DETECTED IN TEST TISSUE.

Mutations? What the hell does that mean?

In answer, my body shudders. Smooth, red bumps erupt up and down my left arm from the injection site, like pimples beneath the surface of my skin. More and more of them appear, growing rapidly and merging together to form enormous, painful super-zits.

The largest of them bursts, spraying the bathroom mirror with pus the same weak yellow shade as the bile I just vomited up.

Several more follow suit, popping and oozing with no provocation but aching like I've been squeezing them for hours. The sensation builds until I collapse on the floor, overcome by the roar of dizziness in my ears.

Abruptly, it stops. The pain. The sound. I feel and hear nothing and wonder if I'm still conscious. If I passed out, would I know?

Then the singing begins, everyone at once. "Happy birthday to you…" they holler in a key unknown to any musician. It's an unholy clamor, but it reminds me why I came here. The sudden return of the weakness in my muscles tells me I have to follow through. Now more than ever, I have a task to cross off my bucket list.

I pull my sleeve down to cover my leaking arm and open the door. For an instant, I panic and draw back into the small bathroom. But nobody is looking at me; they're all facing the other direction, watching a pair of little kids—I assume they're my second cousins—carry a lit birthday cake to my sister.

There's only one name on that cake. No smooshed "Tabatha" to distract from the only person Hannah really cares about. She bares her teeth in a wide, drunken smile and counts the candles.

This is it. The perfect moment. I step into the kitchen, finally able to do what I should have done years ago.

Hannah's face, identical to my own apart from some healthy weight in her cheeks, lifts up from the candles as I walk toward her. She really is beautiful. I'll never understand how her career evaporated the way it did, right when mine took off. But as she recognizes me, the mirth vanishes from her dark eyes. Her jaw clenches, and she raises a shaking hand to point a finger at me.

I open my mouth. The words are there. My apology is ready. Justified though it felt in the moment, I did push her out. It's only fair I bring her back in, and if this drug therapy fails—a possibility that seems more and more likely by the minute—Hannah will get my shares of Twin Helix too.

"Hannah, I'm—" I begin, but she cuts me off.

"You backstabbing bitch," she growls, banging a fist down on the counter beside the cake. The flames atop the candles jiggle, then still.

I'm prepared for this. "Hear me out. I want to apologize. For everything." I hold up my hands, palms out toward her. "I'm here to make it right."

"Make it right?" She sways on her feet, and I realize surprising her while she's drunk might not have been the best timing after all. "There's nothing you can do to make it right, Tabby. But I'm glad you're here. I've been thinking all year about what to wish for on my birthday."

"Whatever you want, I'll give it to you. Anything."

Her eyes narrow. "Yeah, right. Know what I want? I want everything."

I stumble forward, eager to reach her but out of energy. "You can have it!"

"Good. 'Cause here's my wish: I want everything you've got. Everything should be mine." She blows out the candles, then snarls at me. "How's that, huh?"

"You can have it all," I whisper. "Everything is yours."

"Good. Let's start with your pride." She pulls back a fist, readying to punch me over the counter.

I don't flinch. I deserve this. And who knows, maybe she'll knock me out and I won't wake up again. I wouldn't complain. The will has been drawn up and signed. I'll make things right whether she accepts it or not.

Hannah freezes, her smile suddenly emptied of the eager cruelty it held a moment ago. She drops her fist, cradling it with her other hand, and hisses in pain. "What the hell is this?"

As she raises her hand to her face to examine it, scattered bumps appear up and down her arms. They multiply, spreading up her neck.

I realize what's about to happen just in time to duck beneath the counter, moving faster than I have in weeks. My family shrieks in unison as the bumps on Hannah's body explode, showering everyone in the kitchen with milky yellow pus. Something heavy falls to the floor on the other side of the counter.

The pain fades from my body, and I rip back my left sleeve. My arm is fine, smooth and clear. Even the needle marks are gone.

I leap to my feet as the oldsters from the dining room hurry to Hannah's side. I'm not sure if I should help or not, just as I'm not sure if Twin Helix will still be in my name when I get back to the office.

Truth is, I don't really care. Thanks to my sister, I have my health.

She can have the rest.

THE FISHERMEN

Z oe's feet hurt. Her toes strained against the fronts of her too-small hiking boots, and an angry blister was growing on the ball of her left foot. It'd started while they'd been searching for food on their way out of the canyon, and by the time Topher led her up a steep gulley toward an abandoned subdivision in the foothills, she was wincing with every step.

"You doing okay?" Topher asked over his shoulder, his voice low.

"I'm fine."

"Liar." Topher widened the gap between them, leaving her to struggle through the underbrush. "You're slowing down. And your paces are uneven."

She glared at the back of his head, wondering how he could tell.

"You'd hear it too if you were paying attention, runt."

"I *am* paying—"

Topher stopped and held up a hand. "Shut up."

Zoe's first instinct was to argue. If she were back home at the camp and Topher was being this rude, her mother might've had a thing or two to say about it. But she wasn't home. This wasn't their safe, fortified camp. And she was no fool. She knew what could be waiting for them out here. So she shut her mouth, stopped walking, and watched Topher.

Her cousin leaned forward and pushed aside a tree branch. His free hand drifted down to his belt, where one of the camp's four working handguns was tucked. Zoe ran a thumb over the handle of the hunting knife that was clipped to the side of her jeans and shuddered. If he drew that gun... then they weren't alone.

The seconds ticked by. Zoe strained her ears, trying to catch the sound of whatever had alarmed Topher. She heard only rushing water in a nearby stream and a gentle rustling of leaves as the breeze teased her short, dark curls.

At last, Topher's shoulders relaxed. He dropped his hand from his weapon and turned to face her.

"Ready?" he asked.

"For what? What was all that?"

"We're at the road."

Zoe's mouth went dry. She had to swallow before she could ask her next question. "Like, a paved one?"

He nodded. "That's why we had to stop. Lesson one: never leave the canopy without checking for Ogres."

Ogres. They were the reason Zoe's camp was surrounded by spiked logs and pit traps. Why weapons and ammunition were worth more than clean water. And why so many people never made it back to camp alive.

She knew from taking her turn in the watchtowers that Ogres weren't hard to spot. They didn't hide. Her father said they thought it was cowardly.

"They wear bright orange and yellow," he'd told her, "because they want their prey to see them coming."

"Did you see any?" she whispered to Topher.

He shook his head and rolled his eyes. "This really *is* your first time outside of camp, ain't it? If I'd seen any, I wouldn't be talking to you right now, dip. We'd be hiding."

A spark of anger burned in Zoe's stomach. How dare he treat her like a child? She was fifteen, old enough to be trusted with finding food and supplies. Topher was only two years older than her and acted like he knew everything, but she was smarter than him. At least she knew that *ain't* wasn't even a word.

She opened her mouth to tell him as much but closed it again when she saw him grinning.

"Still afraid?" he asked.

"I—" She wasn't. Her indignation had wiped out her fear. "No. I'm not."

"Good. Anger is better. Come on."

THE NEIGHBORHOOD looked different from the ones in Zoe's memories. Lush green lawns perfect for games of tag, smooth sidewalks that led her to school and back, well-tended gardens up and down the block—whether it was her own street or her grandmother's, those things were standard. Constant. Normal.

None of those were present here. Tall grasses and wild saplings had taken over every yard in the five years since the evacuation. She could still make out the colored stucco on most of the houses, but the structures were damaged from fallen trees and roving animals. Broken windows, cars with flat tires, and roofs with gaping holes peppered the block.

"It's awful," she whispered.

Topher heard her. He heard everything.

"Ain't that bad. I've seen worse. These ones might have food storage still." He led her up a curving driveway to a large two-story house, stopping on the front porch. "Look, there's a skateboard over there."

She followed his pointing finger with her eyes. He was right; the weathered wood of a longboard was sticking up from the grass in the yard. She walked over to it and knelt to dig it out of the ground, wondering if she could salvage it for getting down the mountain faster next time.

Someone had scratched something into the wood. She brushed away a bit of ground-in dirt to read it.

CANDACE – R.I.P. 2018

Zoe hopped to her feet and scurried back to Topher.

"It's a headstone," she whispered.

He shrugged. "Won't be the last one you see, I bet."

"They buried people right in their yard?" She thought of her family's dog, Ruffles, who'd been laid to rest in the flower patch by their garage when she was nine. "Like animals?"

"They had to put 'em all somewhere." He cocked his head to one side and raised a blond eyebrow at her. "You were, what, ten when it happened? Don't you remember?"

She nodded, but she wasn't sure she had the memories he was asking for. Every cell phone in her classroom ringing at once with an alert about the attacks on the east coast. Huddling in the gym with the rest of her elementary school until her parents came to get her in the big pickup truck with their camping trailer in tow. She never saw her house again, her room with the white-and-pink striped walls.

Topher snorted suddenly, dragging her back into the present.

"Oh right, I almost forgot," he said. "Your daddy's the Sergeant. You were probably safe up at the camp before the virus even crossed the state line."

She didn't bother confirming it. Everyone in the camp knew her father had been prepping for the end of the world while most people were just watching TV dramas about it.

Topher tried the doorknob, then kicked the bottom of the door when it didn't budge. He turned to Zoe and held out a hand. "Here, you got your crowbar handy?"

ZOE WANTED to leave the house five minutes after Topher busted in the door. The air was too still, but dust managed to tickle the inside of her nose. Silence lay over the place like a thick quilt, and the eyes of the light-haired family who'd lived here seemed to follow her from the photos on the living room walls.

"I don't like it here."

"Tough. This is the best bet we've got. Big family like this probably had camping gear and lots of food in the pantry."

"Maybe they took it with them to a camp like ours."

He snorted again. The sound made Zoe want to punch him.

"These folks weren't working class like us. Look here." He tapped a black-framed diploma over a desk against the wall. "This guy was a doctor. They probably got a golden ticket to a government refuge. Now come on, I think the kitchen's this way."

Topher proved to be right. The pantry was full of canned produce, dried pasta, and even a huge bag of Halloween candy. Everything was at least three years past its expiration date, but they'd long since stopped caring. She and Topher made a pinky promise not to tell her father about the candy, ripped it open, and sat down inside the pantry to gorge for a few happy minutes. The stale chocolate didn't quite melt in her mouth the way she remembered, but it tasted better than anything she'd had in ages.

"Is this why nobody ever manages to bring candy back to camp? They just hog it all?"

Topher grinned, his square teeth coated with brown. "Hey, we're the ones out here taking all the risks. A little candy ain't a lot to ask in return."

Zoe stood up and brushed her hands off on her jeans. "What's next?"

"We gotta check the basement and the garage. Sometimes there's a separate space for the serious food storage. Sometimes we get lucky and find sleeping bags or fishing rods."

She smiled at the thought of bringing fishing supplies back to her father. He loved to fish and always said it was more fun than hunting.

"You think we'll find some bait?" She elbowed Topher.

That earned her a chuckle and a pat on the head. "We'll just have to wait and see."

They walked back to the house's entryway where a curved wooden banister drew Zoe's eyes to the top floor. To her side, a second staircase led down to the basement.

"Hey…" Zoe stared up at the landing above them. "You think the bedrooms are up there?"

"Probably. Why?"

She wiggled her toes in her tattered boots, cringing as her raw feet rubbed against the thin inner soles. "I need new shoes. Bad. Can we take a look?"

Topher turned and stared out the wide front windows. The sun was still high in the sky, but it was creeping steadily toward the western horizon. He pursed his lips, and Zoe held her breath.

He nodded. "Okay. Let's make it quick."

Up the stairs and through an open door on her left, Zoe found a lavender-painted bedroom. The boy-band posters on the walls convinced her she'd find shoes fit for a teenage girl before she even threw open the double-wide closet. She squealed when she saw knee-high boots that could be her size and tossed a grin over her shoulder at Topher.

He frowned down at his own worn tennis shoes, then tugged at the bottom of the oversize camo jacket he'd borrowed from Zoe's father. "Smart move, cuz. I'm gonna check the master bedroom for anything that might fit me."

The image of Topher trying to move stealthily through the trees in a suit and tie flashed into her mind, and she couldn't help but giggle as he left the room. "*Suit* yourself," she called.

She tried on every pair of shoes she could find. They were all a half size too small, but she didn't give up. She pawed through the clothes hanging above her, looking for anything she could bring back to camp.

A loud thump sounded from downstairs, like a door being flung open by the wind.

Or by an Ogre.

She nearly called out to Topher to see if he'd gone downstairs without her, but her father's instructions rang in her mind as clearly as when he'd been hammering them into her that morning.

"If you get separated, don't call out," he'd said. "Topher won't be the only thing out there with ears."

Taking care not to let the hangers clink together, she let her hands fall away from the clothing. Then she backed into the closet and closed the folding doors in front of her, stopping just before they clicked into place. A thin crack remained. She shuffled to the side, peered out through the horizontal slats in the doors, and waited.

Her heart pounded in her ears, blocking out any chance of hearing footsteps on the stairs.

"Over here," someone said from the hallway. It was a man's voice, deep and gruff like her father's, but there was no warmth in it.

Zoe raised her hands to her face and clamped them tightly over her mouth to keep from screaming. If they found her…

She didn't let herself finish the thought. She wouldn't be able to keep that scream inside if she did.

"You think there's somebody in here?" a second voice said, louder and higher pitched than the first but still male.

"Scratch marks on the front door don't lie. Somebody definitely broke in here. Scavengers, maybe."

"Mmm-mmm." The second voice made a slurping sound. "Haven't had me a good meal in weeks."

Their footsteps creaked in the hallway, and through the slats in her closet door Zoe, saw the men pass by the lavender bedroom.

One was tall with broad shoulders. The second followed behind like a wispy shadow. Both wore bright yellow hunting vests. If she'd seen these same two men in her camp, they would've been just that: men. But out here, in those colors, they were something else entirely.

Ogres.

Her stomach lurched. They were headed right for Topher. Could she warn him?

She didn't have time. They were already in the master bedroom.

If she'd heard them, Topher heard them. Maybe he'd gotten out.

Zoe stood, shivering, clutching her mouth and trying not to think about the beads of sweat that dripped between her shoulder blades. If the fireside legends were true and Ogres could smell fear, she wouldn't be able to hide in this closet for long.

From the master bedroom, she heard the sounds of drawers opening, followed by heavy thumps.

"Check the closet," the deep voice said.

A door opened, and she heard loud rummaging.

"Nothing," called back the high voice.

"There's somebody here. I can feel it."

There was a loud creaking, then a crash and a scream. She'd never heard Topher make a noise that sounded that scared before, but it was him. Her fingernails dug into her cheekbones.

A gunshot rang out.

"Ooo-eee!" screeched the man with the high voice. "We got us a live wire here, Clem!"

"We sure do," said Clem. "What are you thinking, boy? You can't aim worth a damn with a broken arm. Give me that."

She heard a second gunshot, and Topher screamed again.

"That hurt?" asked Clem. "Just you wait, son. You alone?"

She heard a gurgling sound, like somebody rinsing their mouth out in the river. Was that Topher?

"Come on, now. You can do better than that. Who's with you? Your daddy?"

A pause.

"Good. Don't worry, we won't hurt him. Where is he?"

Another pause.

"What the hell is that supposed to mean?"

"I think the garage," said the high-pitched voice. "See? He's driving an invisible car, there."

"Did Grayson solve the puzzle?" Clem asked, raising his voice. "Are we gonna find your daddy down in that garage?"

Silence followed. Then a third gunshot.

Someone grunted.

"Kid weighs a ton," said Grayson.

"No sense trying to carry him out like that. You break him down. I'll check the garage and find a tarp to carry him back with."

"And hopefully his daddy too," Grayson said with a high laugh.

Bile rose in Zoe's mouth. Topher was dead. She knew it with a dull certainty. But fear for her own life outweighed any sorrow she could feel for her cousin right now. He was already gone, and as far as Ogres were concerned, he'd gotten lucky. His death had been quick.

Her father never skimped the details when he told stories at camp gatherings. Ogres didn't just eat people; they tortured them. Raped them. The Ogre camp was a haven for people who were happy the world had ended. People who'd abandoned their humanity and reveled in becoming monsters.

The broad-shouldered man, who must be Clem, passed by the teenage girl's bedroom toward the stairs. Zoe took a tiny breath through her fingers, then held it again.

Creak.

Zoe's eyes widened as Clem passed back in front of the lavender bedroom, stopped in the doorway, and stared around the room. His heavy-lidded eyes focused on every piece of furniture, every poster on the wall, and then on the nearly closed doors that concealed her.

She stared at him through the slats, unable to look away or even blink. No air escaped her lungs, but she was certain he would hear her heart pounding against her sternum.

Please, God, if you're up there... don't let him find me.

After another visual pass of the room, Clem turned around and left the doorway. She heard heavy footsteps clomping down the stairs and dared to breathe again. She let her hands drop to her sides and flexed her fingers in and out of tight fists.

A series of wet thumps and loud cracks sounded from the master bedroom. She squeezed her eyes closed. There was nothing she could do for Topher now. She had to look out for herself.

Inch by inch, with one hand on the hinges and the other curled around the edge of the door, Zoe opened one side of the closet just enough to slink out into the bedroom. She paused inside the threshold to the hallway and weighed her options.

To her left, Grayson was butchering her cousin. Somewhere to her right and below her, Clem was probably figuring out that nobody was in the garage. Would he assume Topher had been telling the truth and that his father had cut and run when he heard the gunshots? Maybe he wouldn't bother searching the house, and she could get out. Or would he sense that Topher had been lying and comb through every hiding place he could think of?

Either way, he'd be coming back to Grayson soon to help haul off Topher's body.

Zoe didn't like the idea of Clem finding her huddled in some cabinet or under a bed. She needed to get out of the house. And she couldn't risk meeting him on the stairs with nothing but her hunting knife. Her only chance to escape alive was somewhere in that master bedroom.

She needed Topher's gun.

Knife in hand and back against the wall, Zoe crept down the hallway. She ran her thumb down the well-worn handle of the weapon, drawing comfort from the fact that the blade was so old. It meant the people who'd taken it outside the camp before her had come back alive. She imagined those people beside her now, supporting her.

It was a little easier to walk into battle once she didn't feel alone.

She took care not to shuffle her feet against the carpet, but she couldn't be sure she was successful. Despite the company of her imaginary compatriots, her traitorous heart was booming in her ears again.

Slowly, the master bedroom came into view through the open doorway. Grayson's slender back was to her, and he appeared to be completely engrossed in his gruesome task. Zoe squeezed her eyes shut for a brief second, just long enough to beg herself not to lose consciousness at the sight of the blood-covered floor. Then she opened her eyes, gripped her knife in both hands, and leaped through the doorway.

Her aim wasn't bad, and she'd thrown her entire weight behind it. The blade plunged deep between Grayson's shoulders with a wet *shick*. She gritted her teeth and leaned down onto the handle for good measure.

He inhaled sharply, shuddered, and slumped forward onto what remained of Topher's body. Zoe gripped her knife and panted for a moment, then swallowed back the bile that was creeping up her throat before searching for Topher's gun amid the gore.

"Looking for this?"

Clem's deep voice made her jump, and she spun around to face the doorway. He was standing there with a twisted grin on his ruddy face, dangling the small handgun from between two fingers.

He whistled approvingly. "Not too bad, little girl. You one of them Goblins that lives up Farmington Canyon?"

She stared at him, eyes wide and palms sweaty. "We don't like that name."

"Oh? And what do you prefer to be called?"

"Fishermen."

Clem laughed. "This ain't a world for fishermen, girly. Takin' it easy at the lakeside, drinkin' a beer, waitin' around for the fish to bite. You wanna survive? You gotta hunt."

A glint of light danced on the wall just behind Clem's head. It flashed once, paused, and flashed twice again.

"You're wrong," she said, a smile spreading over her face. "You have to do both."

"Wha—"

Zoe heard the noise again, the soggy *shick* of a knife cutting through a man's back. Clem's eyes bugged out. He stiffened for a moment before deflating and crumpling to the floor.

Zoe's father stood in the doorway, a bloodied blade in his hand.

"Good girl," he whispered.

She stood on the front porch beside her father, arms wrapped around herself, and watched as several men from the camp loaded Clem, Grayson, and Topher onto the backs of large all-terrain vehicles.

"You were late," she said. She turned toward her father and buried her face in his chest. "They killed Topher."

"I know, honey." He stroked the back of her head with a calloused hand. "The truck broke down at the bottom of the canyon. We had to go back for the four-wheelers."

One of the men was struggling to tie down Clem's large body. It was quite the haul; they could make enough jerky to feed the whole camp for a week.

Her father clucked her under the chin with one curled forefinger. "Hey, you know how much we hate to lose someone. But this is the world we live in."

She nodded. It was the risk they took every time they went scavenging, coming in on foot and leaving obvious marks on the doors of the homes they searched. The live bait didn't always survive.

"You know," he said, "before all this happened, I thought there was nothing better than a quiet day at the lake. I lived to fish."

She'd heard this before. It was his mantra, what he said to every person who was drafted to leave the camp. She finished the chant for him.

"And now we fish to live."

THE DEVIL'S WAY OUT

The demon is here. Here to collect.

I know he's in my parlor before I open my eyes. The foul stench of freshly brewed peppermint tea tickles my nostrils and triggers my gag reflex.

He's warped that smell, stolen something I used to love and twisted it against me. If the demon accomplishes nothing else—and I pray that's the case—I'll hate him to my grave for destroying my fondness for my favorite tea.

The fresh, sweet scent of peppermint used to mean we were finished with our chores for the day. We'd come in from clearing the snow off our farmhouse's wide porch or mucking out the horses' stalls, and Mama would have a big pot of peppermint tea waiting for me on the table. My little brothers preferred hot chocolate, but I liked the tea. Mama said it made me dignified.

I kept the tradition for years after that, rewarding myself after a day of studying for my exams with a steaming pot. Then, when Papa got sick, teatime meant my turn to sit by his bedside. I'm thankful for that. It made me feel like spending time with him, even on his deathbed, was a reward. A good thing. And it gave me somewhere to hide my nose, near the end, when the sickroom took on the telltale odor of approaching death.

Now, as I stare down at the steaming mug that suddenly appeared on my coffee table, my lip curls into what I'm sure is an unflattering sneer. I hate that smell now, because it means the demon has dropped by for one of his little visits.

Sure enough, when I raise my head, I see him sitting in the wingback chair across from me. The curtains behind him are drawn, blocking out the afternoon sunlight. He's dressed like a banker, in a slim gray suit, white shirt, and narrow black tie. It seems an appropriate choice to me, given how many times the bank tried to snatch our land away from us in the slow years, when season after season of drought devastated our crops. Pure evil, that's what they were. And all of them dressed like this demon.

"How are you today?" Timothy asks.

That isn't his name. His real name is probably Vual or Barbatos or some other foul word, but he'll never tell me what it is. No, that'd give me too much power over him. Papa warned me about that. When I asked the demon his name, he lied. He gave me Papa's name instead of the truth. Stole that right along with Papa's lean, narrow face and his light blue eyes. It's just one of the tricks he likes to play in his attempts to torment me.

I huff out through my nose and set the novel I've been reading down on the table beside the mug. "Save your breath. You don't care about me."

A pained smile flashes across the demon's face. I like that smile. It means my plan is working. I'm wearing the demon down, just like Papa told me to.

The demon sits in silence for a while, his hands folded in his lap, watching me. Sizing me up. I straighten up in my chair and dust off the folds of my skirt, determined to look dignified. For Mama. She's probably looking down at me from heaven right now, and I hope she's proud. I'm standing my ground, just like she did—a tall, lean woman in a dark gray dress, warding off the bankers with a shotgun in her hand.

The demon sighs. "I don't know why you're being so difficult. You know this is the best thing for you. Sign on the dotted line, and everything will be so much easier."

"I'd rather die." It's the truth. If I die, the deal dies with me. I'm a bit young for it—only twenty after all. But I haven't married yet. I have no children to pass this curse along to, the way Papa passed it to me. If that's what it comes to, I'll take the path gladly.

Timothy stands up, pulls on a pair of black leather gloves, and heads for the door. "I'll be back tomorrow," he promises.

As soon as the door clicks shut behind him, I get up to dump out the untouched mug, wishing he'd for once do me the courtesy of making the tea disappear as efficiently as he conjured it in the first place. I come back into the parlor and throw open the curtains, letting some light into the room. A few feet across the alleyway, there's a gray brick building, beyond which lies a great big park with trees and a gazebo. I'll admit it'd be nice to have some greenery to gaze at when I'm feeling cooped up, but this apartment is the first place that's *mine*. I paid for it with the money from Papa's life insurance, decorated it, and made it into a home. And truth be told, I have the best view in the city.

The curtain across the alley twitches before being drawn back by a large hand. I smile across the way at my neighbor, Duncan. He's a tall man with a wide build, a pillar of strength who would've towered over even my Papa. Duncan lifts open his window, and I do the same.

"Hey there, Letha." His green eyes sparkle so brightly they light up the entire world. "Feeling hungry?"

"Starving." I pat my bangs down, hoping my lipstick hasn't smudged since this morning.

"There's a new Chinese restaurant just down the street." He leans his thick, muscled arms against the bottom frame of his window so that his head and shoulders poke out into the alley. "I don't suppose I could tempt you outside for some dim sum?"

I bite my lip. Duncan could tempt me into doing a lot of things, and I hope there are lots of things he ends up tempting me into. But going outside isn't one of them. "I don't suppose they do takeout?"

He shoots me a grin and a wink. "Coming right up."

After closing my window, I glance over at the faded black-and-yellow photos of my parents that hang above the fireplace mantel. Their serious, thin-lipped faces are filled with concern for my welfare.

"Don't worry," I tell them. "I'm staying inside."

I'M KNITTING in my favorite armchair by the fire. I blink, and upon opening my eyes, three things have changed: the shades are drawn, the demon is sitting across from me, and the whole room reeks of that damn peppermint tea.

It's been three weeks since Timothy last visited.

"Tomorrow, huh?" I say.

"What?" He's staring around the room, frowning at the decor. I don't see what's so wrong with it. The walls are papered with bright blue forget-me-nots, and paperbacks tightly pack the pair of bookcases that flank the fireplace. I always keep the apartment nice and tidy; it feels bigger when it's clean. Of course, like any place, it looks much better with an abundance of natural light, but the demon isn't having any of that.

There's a knock at the door, and a second man enters. This

one looks even more like a banker than Timothy, which I hadn't thought possible. His suit is a deep black, and a short goatee covers his chin. I want to laugh, expecting to see a pointed red tail sneak up from behind the second demon's shoulder. They're getting lazy about hiding their true forms.

The new demon pulls out a crisp, new copy of the contract and offers it to me. "Come now, be reasonable." His voice is deep and smooth as silk, dripping with seduction. "I think you'll find the terms very generous."

A short, incredulous bark erupts from my mouth. "Generous? Generous would be if you let me keep my soul."

The demons shift in their seats, clearly uncomfortable with my candor. I'm sure they're not used to humans, especially women, speaking to them so directly. But they should know better. After all, they knew my Papa.

On his deathbed, Papa told me the whole story. When I was eight, the farm was failing. The bankers wouldn't stop coming, even though Mama sent a very clear message with her shotgun, and we teetered on the edge of ruin.

That's when Papa had his Very Bad Idea. Oh, his intentions were good. And I'm not sure we would've survived if he hadn't done what he did. He went down to the crossroads and made a deal with a demon. They agreed that if the demon could help the farm survive, he could take Papa's soul.

But Papa was clever. He wheezed and cackled when he told me all about the sneaky thing he did, how he made sure the demon could only take him if he died in water. And there he was, dying high and dry from pneumonia instead. Oh, Papa would crow and crow about that. And I'd chuckle too, between sips of my peppermint tea.

The memory makes me giggle now, and that giggle turns into a great whooping laugh. Before long, I'm laughing so hard that I start to cough, and I double over in my chair. I reach for the mug of tea from the table, but it's gone. So are the demons. They've left me alone in my sunlit parlor, coughing without an audience.

TIMOTHY IS BACK AGAIN, looking worse than ever. His suit is wrinkled, and his face is covered in short, graying stubble. It's an odd look; my father never went gray. He died while his hair was still thick and black. Timothy is really slipping now. He must be downright desperate. He's even forgotten to summon a steaming cup of peppermint tea.

I'd be worried, if he weren't trying to steal my soul.

"Come with me," he says. "Let's just go outside for one minute."

I shake my head, a rueful smile on my lips. "You know better than that, Timothy," I tell him. Outside, there's water. I settled in a landlocked state for safety, in a city far away from any lakes, but I've heard rain on my window in recent days. I can't risk slipping and falling into a puddle. I'm certain even an inch of water would meet the demon's conditions, and I'd much rather hang on to my soul, thank you very much.

"I don't care if I don't leave this apartment until I'm old and gray," I tell him, lifting my chin and pointing at the drawn curtains. "And even then, they'll have to carry me out in a pine box."

"This is ridiculous!" Timothy shouts, shedding the last of his bankerly demeanor. He lunges across the room and grabs my arm.

When his fingertips touch my skin, my vision goes black. Something heavy presses against my chest, and I can't draw a full breath. I gasp and claw at the nothing around me, searching for anything to grab on to. Cold racks my body, forcing my muscles to contract before a sudden heat presses in all around me, and my muscles expand until each and every one strains at my skin, threatening to escape my body.

"Stop," I moan, begging for relief. "Stop!"

The pain relents, giving way to a dull ache. I'm able to breathe again, and I suck in air, blinking rapidly against the darkness. A pinprick of light sparks to life somewhere in front of me, and I follow it. Not with my body—my limbs are locked in place, stuck to the floor like they've been nailed there. Timothy won't let me get up, but he has something to show me: a vision of the apocalypse.

I'm standing atop my apartment building and surveying the destruction in the city around me. All I can see in any direction is ruin and rubble, and I scan desperately for Duncan's building. It's gone. There's nothing more than a pile of gray stones across the alley. Timothy's face floats above me, taunting me from the sky.

He did this. I can feel it in my bones.

"Leave me alone!" I scream. My voice stretches strangely with nothing to echo against, but it repeats anyway, the words growing in volume until they're all I can hear, my own shrill and frightened voice trapped in an endless loop.

The vision dissipates. The colors swirl, and I see him: Duncan. My anchor. His red-bearded face and light green eyes smile down at me from the sky above, sending comfort. Sending love.

"I'm here," he whispers.

"Duncan," I breathe.

His presence gives me the strength to break free of Timothy's spell. I wake up back in my armchair, curled up and crying. Then I remember the destruction in my vision, and I force myself out of my seat to pull back the curtains. Duncan's building is still there, the gray stones shimmering with the faint slick of rain. I sink to the floor and wrap my arms around my torso, staring at his window until the throbbing pain—the last remnant of Timothy's punishment—subsides.

I'M DOZING LIGHTLY in my parlor when the stink of peppermint jolts me awake. Timothy is standing in front of the fireplace, examining the photographs of my parents.

"You're back," I croak. I clear my throat to chase the sleep out of my voice.

He turns to face me, and he looks a little less haggard than the last time he was here. But his eyelids still sag, and large bags darken his face.

Good, I think, remembering the aches and pains I suffered for days after his last visit.

He sucks in a deep breath, peering around the apartment with that expression of naked disdain he always seems to wear. I don't blame him for hating this place. These walls are all that keep him from reaching his goal.

I wonder what would happen to him if he managed to collect on Papa's contract, so I ask, "Where will you go when this is over?"

"I'll be with you." There's an odd note in his voice, almost like he's trying to reassure me.

I raise my eyebrows. It's so pitiful; he thinks this will end with my soul in Hell, so he can torment me for all eternity. Well, not if I have anything to say about it.

"And if I'm in Heaven?" I taunt him. "What will you do then?"

He turns his head in disgust and goes back to glaring at the photo of my father in the dim light.

"Admiring your costume?" I ask. "Well, you'll see it much better in the light."

I stand, march over to the window, and yank the curtains open. It's a beautiful morning outside, and the sun reflects off Duncan's building to fill the whole parlor with daylight. I push up the window to let in the sounds and smells of springtime, then turn back to Timothy to see how he likes it when I chase away all his doom and gloom.

But Timothy is gone. His instincts are too good.

"Hey, gorgeous," I hear from behind me.

Duncan is leaning out his window again, a smile on his face and a spatula in his hand. "I'm making breakfast. I'll put in it a big dish and bring it over in a few minutes, okay?"

My heart swells in my chest, and I blow Duncan a kiss.

I wonder how he'd feel about moving across the alley.

TIMOTHY GIVES me no warning the next time he appears. No mug. No tea. He doesn't even bother to draw the curtains. I just blink and he's there, sitting across the coffee table from me with my coat in his hands. For the first time ever, light from the window shines onto him, illuminating him like a spotlight. I notice he has flecks of red in his hair, which is longer than I've ever seen it. His face is pale, and if I thought demons ever slept, I'd say he was in desperate need of a solid eight hours.

"It's time," he tells me.

I stiffen in my chair. There's a finality in his voice, laced with a deep and troubling sadness.

Something is different.

Something is wrong.

Now I see the evidence of his latest trick. The photographs

of my parents are missing, and my bookshelves have been emptied.

"What did you do with them?" I demand, struggling to my feet. My limbs are numb with fear and anger.

Timothy shakes his head, and for some reason, tears spill down his cheeks. "You packed them," he said. "Remember?"

Rage builds in my chest until my vision grows fuzzy. Lies on top of lies, that's all the demon knows.

A knock sounds, and Timothy opens the door. Two men enter the apartment—large men, like Duncan. But there's no laughter in their eyes. No flirtatious twinkle. Timothy nods at them, and they bear down on me, each of them grabbing one of my arms. I scream and thrash, trying to break their grip, but they're impossibly strong.

I realize they're demons, not men. Just as Timothy has the power to make things appear and disappear, these demons possess an inhuman strength. They haul me toward the door, intending to drag me out of the apartment by force, and there's nothing I can do to stop them.

Not on my own.

"Duncan!" I scream his name so loudly that it rips and burns my throat. "DUNCAN!" I twist around, trying to see out my window.

It's closed. Duncan can't hear me.

"Stop," Timothy tells the men. "She needs to see."

Their grips loosen slightly, and they take me to the window. The curtains are pulled back, and sunlight streams in.... So much sunlight....

Too much sunlight.

"What is this?" I whisper.

The view out my window is unrecognizable. Duncan's building is gone; I can see the park that lies beyond it. The demons release me, and I stumble to the window, barely able to keep myself upright from shock. The ground below is covered in piles of gray bricks, just like in my vision.

I grab the curtains on each side of me, clutching them for strength. "You did this," I rasp, my voice ruined from my earlier scream. I clench my fists, squeezing the heavy fabric in each hand. "You did this!"

Timothy stands beside me. I can see his reflection in the glass from my periphery but can't bear to look directly at him.

"Your building is next," he says. "You have no choice anymore. You have to leave."

I squeeze my eyes closed and shake my head vigorously, hoping to banish this hallucination. I've beaten them before. But when I open my eyes, the rubble is still there.

This is no vision.

This is real.

Sorrow, anger, and defeat bear down on me, buckling my knees. My grip on the curtains loosens, and I cry out as I fall to the floor.

Someone pulls me into their arms. They're shaking, and wet droplets spatter against my skin.

"Duncan," I whisper. "You came."

I pull back and cup his face in my hands, then recoil. Timothy is cradling me. His features are contorted in sadness, and tears stream down his cheeks.

"I'm so sorry," he tells me, tugging me close again. "Mom, I am so sorry."

Four strong hands grab me from behind, and I'm dragged away from him. His weeping form, backlit by the window behind him, is achingly familiar.

The light fills my vision, then flashes like lightning. My skull threatens to split open, my mind unable to contain the sudden swell of memories that cascade into it like a lake below a broken dam.

I see Timothy there, crying beside that same window. I'm standing beside him. We're gazing across the alleyway, remembering all the times Timothy's father leaned across it to flirt with me. I'm telling Timothy about the day Duncan threw me a rose tied to a piece of string. When I caught it, he used the string to slide a diamond ring from his window to mine. I'm telling Timothy these stories to distract him, to distract myself, because the mortuary staff are in the bedroom, preparing to take Duncan out of the apartment, and we all know I won't be able to bring myself to follow him out the door.

Timothy is crying at the window again, begging me to leave the building. To go live with him and his wife in their new house in the suburbs. But I can't; I have too many memories here. This is where I met Duncan. Where we courted. Where we made love, where we conceived our son. Where we raised our boy. Where I battled—and was defeated by—my fear of the outside world again and again over the years.

And now, for the last time, my son sobs by the window overlooking the development project that finally forced his hand. Finally forced *my* hand. I *did* sign the papers. I *did* pack my boxes, all while drinking my favorite peppermint tea.

But how long ago?

And how many times?

I go limp, and the men carry me over the threshold. The door swings closed behind us, and I can't bear it. I can't handle seeing my apartment from the outside, especially knowing I'll never see the inside of it again.

I'll never seen my Duncan again.

I close my eyes, squeezing them tightly against the disappearing light, and beg for mercy. Some way, any way, to stop this waking nightmare from becoming my life.

When I open them again, there's a steaming cup of tea sitting on the coffee table in my parlor. Timothy sits across from me, a sad smile on his face as he gazes around at my floral wallpaper. I glare at him, wrinkling my nose at the peppermint stench.

The demon is here. Here to collect.

FAMILY TIME

Maeve hated Great-Aunt Phyllis's house the minute she saw it. She didn't need the Mylar balloons flapping around the front door to tell her who lived here; there was an innate wrongness to the place that marked it as being connected to her mother's side of the family.

In fairness, she probably would have hated it no matter what it looked like. She'd had plans that weekend that had nothing to do with getting stuck in a car for four hours with her mother just to attend some old woman's birthday party. In fact, at that very moment, she should have been packing for her first middle school slumber party. But Tara played the "I never exercise my custody rights, you owe me this" card and—despite Maeve's many loud protests, threats, and tears—her father gave in.

"It'll be good for you to get to know your mom," he said.

Maeve would have preferred a day at the park or a night at the roller rink. She didn't see why they had to go to an entirely different state. And Tara hadn't wanted to talk much in the car unless it was about Great-Aunt Phyllis and all her money.

Maeve wiped her nose on her sleeve and tried to figure out why the old woman's house unnerved her so much. Maybe it was the way the building was half as wide and twice as tall as the surrounding homes, or the way it sagged to one side like it was exhausted and needed to take a quick nap on the house next door. The few windows were too small, the roof was too steep, and no other yard had so many stubby little weeds where the lawn should be.

Whatever it was, Maeve didn't want to go inside. She didn't even want to get out of the car, but Tara dragged her onto the sidewalk by her arm.

"Come here. Take off your glasses." Tara cupped her daughter's face in one hand and wielded a damp tissue in the other. "Ugh, you've got tear tracks all over your cheeks. I can't believe you cried that much over a dead skunk."

Maeve sniffed. "You don't know it was dead. You should've pulled over. We could've helped it."

Tara rolled her eyes. "It's a skunk, Maeve. Not everything's worth saving. Now come on. I want you to meet my family."

Four generations had come out for Phyllis's ninetieth birthday, and the house creaked and moaned as the old woman's nieces, nephews, and distant cousins leaned against the walls. Little cousins Maeve had never met ran up and down the stairs leading to the second level, shrieking and playing tag. The older ones, the teenagers who were too cool for family parties, snuck cigarettes on the back patio.

"Who's this, Tara?" everyone asked Maeve's mother.

"My little pride and joy." Tara squeezed Maeve into a sideways hug and tugged her daughter's braided pigtails playfully. "She's in the advanced program at school, you know, on track to get into a great college. We have high hopes for our Maevey."

"Good for you," Aunt Phyllis told Maeve in a reedy voice. "Hard work pays off. You'll see."

When not being introduced to Tara's family, Maeve spent the afternoon perched on a wobbly stool in the kitchen, watching

Phyllis slowly open presents and trying to send telepathic messages to her mother: *Tara Walsh, can you hear me? Get me out of here!*

Not that Tara would have listened. She only had eyes for Phyllis, doting on her elderly aunt, bringing her cake, and helping her manage the knotted ribbons and stubborn tape on the brightly wrapped gifts. Phyllis responded to everything from crayoned birthday cards to a towering, antique grandfather clock with quiet pleasure and a wide, dentured smile.

One of Tara's cousins, a paunchy man in his forties, paused next to Maeve on his way back from grabbing a beer. He popped the top and nodded at the pile of presents. "What'd you get her?"

"Mini slot machine." Maeve pointed to the toy, which Tara had gotten at a rest stop before crossing the border from Nevada. "How about you?"

"That big ugly thing." He tipped his can toward the enormous clock. "Kinda neat, isn't it?"

Neat wasn't the word Maeve had in mind. The clock was tall, even taller than her father, with ornate swirls and leaves carved into the shining black walnut. It was similar in shape to the longcase clock in the vestibule of her school, but this one had solid wood hiding the pendulum instead of clear glass. Like the house, there was something off about the leaning clock, something that sent goose bumps up her arms and left a sour feeling in her stomach. It looked like the kind of thing an evil sorceress would keep in her castle, and if Maeve unfocused her eyes, the decorative flourishes became monstrous faces that scowled down at the party guests.

She hated it.

At least it wasn't ticking. Maeve was impatient enough for this trip to end, and it took all her willpower not to glance at her wristwatch every ten seconds. Happily, the clock was missing its second hand. The spindly minute hand pointed straight up, never moving, and the misshapen hour hand was locked on the elegant, old-fashioned two.

"Neat," she eventually echoed.

"Found it at an estate sale last week. Gave it to a buddy of mine who just retired." A troubled expression clouded his face. "Ended up getting it back though. Thought Aunt Phyllis would like it, you know, since it's probably as old as she is."

Maeve shifted uncomfortably on her stool and pushed her glasses up her nose.

"Anyway, glad to have the thing out of my garage." He eyed the clock and sipped his beer, then shook his head. "Something about it freaks me out."

Maeve didn't answer, and he wandered away. She tried sending messages to Tara through her eyeballs for a few minutes after that, then gave up and slipped off her stool. A longhaired white cat looked like a promising companion for the rest of the party, but it darted away as soon as Maeve approached it, escaping out a small cat flap in the back door. Maeve followed, opening the door and shuffling into the back garden.

There wasn't much space in the narrow yard. The teenagers on the patio glared at her and spread their arms over the deck chairs possessively, so she moped past them and settled onto the rusty swing set in the weeds.

One of the older cousins, a teenager with bleached spiky hair, grinned mischievously as he watched Maeve. He interrupted the surrounding conversations, raising his voice above the others to ask, "You guys hear about Mr. Barnes? That math teacher who just retired?"

"Yeah, he lived across the street from us," the boy next to him said. "He bit it last week. Mom's super upset."

The spiky-haired boy nodded. "Yeah, but do you know *how* he died?"

"Heart attack," someone said.

"Nope, close though. Something scared him to death." A low rumble of disagreement rose but was quickly quieted when Spiky

Hair explained, "They know because he shit himself."

An older girl with purple lipstick rolled her eyes. "Every dead person—"

Spiky Hair coughed and glared at the girl with the lipstick.

She glanced at Maeve, then said, "Makes sense."

"He's not the only one either," Spiky Hair went on. "Old Mrs. Harrington died the week before, remember?"

"And a whole family before that," the girl with the lipstick added. "They said it was a gas leak, but they were lying."

Maeve gripped the chains of her swing, listening intently. She'd known there was something off about this place, but she thought it was just this house or this family. Clearly, there was something terribly wrong with the whole town. She leaned forward, eager to learn more.

"They all died right at midnight," the boy said. "And that's not all they had in common. There's something evil here, and it's hunting down people like *them*. People who"—he paused dramatically, leering at Maeve—"wear *glasses*!"

Maeve's hand unconsciously rose to her own glasses, and she felt the color drain from her cheeks.

Lipstick girl snorted and pointed at her. "Look, the kid's terrified." She raised her voice, calling, "It's a joke, dumbass. Don't go shitting yourself over it."

The group burst into laughter. Just then, a few adults came outside to collect their children. The party was finally over.

Maeve decided she'd had more than enough family time for a while. She was optimistic Tara would drive them straight back to Las Vegas that night, but instead they ended up on a lumpy pullout couch at a cousin's house. At least none of the mean teens from the patio lived there; Maeve was grateful for small blessings.

When they got in the car the next morning, she asked hopefully, "We're going home today, right?"

"One quick stop, sweetie. I just want to spend a little more quality time with Phyllis. She's my favorite aunt, you know, and I'm her favorite niece."

Maeve didn't know. She'd gleaned most of what she knew about Tara from the sporadic afternoon visits that usually coincided with picking up an alimony check. The rest had been filled in by her father's muttered complaints when he thought Maeve wasn't listening. Until Tara proposed this trip, Maeve had never heard of Aunt Phyllis, let alone expected to meet her. But for the second time in two days, she was being dragged to Phyllis's creepy old house.

Tara parked her battered Ford Tempo against the curb and checked her makeup in the rearview mirror. "Just talk about your school and where you want to go to college, okay? Be friendly. Maybe mention how expensive the books will be."

Maeve frowned. College was years away, a vague certainty she could dream about without bothering with the details. "How expensive are they?"

"Very," Tara said.

As Tara strode toward the house, a queasy feeling built up in Maeve's belly. For a moment, she thought she might throw up, and her feet refused to cross the weedy yard. Maeve couldn't decide which would be worse: going into that crumbling death trap or vomiting all over the sidewalk.

A shrill scream split the air before she could make up her mind.

The scream sounded again. It was Tara.

Maeve's visions of the building collapsing in on itself were instantly replaced by the image of her mother fighting for her life against a deranged murderer, and she ran for the door. Inside, she found Tara fumbling with a phone over Great-Aunt Phyllis's body. Maeve's feet carried her forward until she stood at the old woman's side, and her eyes refused to blink, drying out behind her glasses.

Even with blurred vision, she still saw more than she was ready to see.

Phyllis lay on the ground in the middle of her living room. Presents—the jewelry, the lotions, the handmade trinkets—littered the floor. Her glassy eyes stared lifelessly up at the grandfather clock, and her mouth hung open as though she'd been in the middle of a scream when the last of her breath ran out.

The stench of urine and feces rushed into Maeve's sinuses as she sucked in a gasp. She doubled over, coughing, and remembered the conversation on the patio the day before. She knew what had happened here. The smell proved it.

Phyllis had been frightened to death.

Maeve bolted from the house. As she sat in the car, watching family, paramedics, and mortuary staff stream in and out of the building, she tried to force herself to forget what she'd seen. Every time she closed her eyes, she saw Phyllis on the floor, in the shadow of the grandfather clock. The solution, she was sure, was to go home as quickly as possible and pretend they never came.

Tara had other ideas.

"I just want to see her get laid to rest." Tears streamed down Tara's face as she gripped her daughter's shoulders that afternoon. Her nails dug painfully into Maeve's skin. "I'm the closest thing to a daughter she had. She'd want me to be here."

Maeve called her father on Tara's cousins' kitchen phone. She was sure he would agree with her that Tara needed to bring her home now. School was starting in a week; she needed to get ready.

"I wish I could, but I can't make her bring you back." Her father sighed into the phone. "You'll understand when you're older."

They stayed two more nights on the hide-a-bed. Finally, after the eulogies, toasts, and burial were behind them, Tara packed their bags into the Tempo. It was after her bedtime, but Maeve didn't care. In four hours, she would be back in her own bed, and that was worth staying up for.

But Tara didn't drive to the interstate. She took them in the wrong direction, back to Phyllis's house yet again. Headlights off, she cruised past the crooked old building at a low speed before parking the car around the corner.

"You said we were going home." Maeve glared at Tara.

"We are, sweetie. I promise. Right after this." Tara got out of the car. When Maeve didn't follow, she turned back to her daughter and rested her hands on her hips. "Come with me and I'll buy you a Slurpee when we're done."

"I'm okay," Maeve called through the open window. "I'm not supposed to have sugar this late."

"Well, then try this on for size: you get in that house right now, or I'll leave you here and let your father figure out a way to get you home."

"Farts," Maeve muttered, then did as she was told.

At the front door, Tara jiggled the handle a few times and swore. "Hank must've locked it. Phyllis never bothered, but that old coot doesn't trust anybody. Come around back."

They looped around to the patio, and Tara ruffled her daughter's hair. "Can you fit through that kitty door? Unlock the bolt for Mommy?"

Maeve wanted to protest, but Tara's threat from a few minutes before still rang in her ears. Quietly, she lowered herself to the ground and fit her shoulders through the flap covering the little rectangular hole at the bottom of the kitchen door. She was small for eleven, shorter and thinner than most of the other girls in her grade. She slipped easily through the cat flap and, for a moment, stood alone inside Aunt Phyllis's house.

The darkness around her was nearly complete. Only the microwave's digital display lit the kitchen, and the pale green glow didn't come close to chasing the shadows from the corners. Maeve's eyes fixed on the darkest part of the room—the little space between the purring refrigerator and the stairs leading to the basement. She froze, unable to move or breathe, sure the evil thing the teenagers had been talking about was waiting for her there, licking its lips as it watched its prey.

A light tap sent a bolt of lightning down Maeve's back.

"Let me in!" Tara hissed from outside.

Without taking her eyes off the corner where the monster waited, Maeve reached behind herself and unlocked the door.

"About time," Tara whispered when she stepped inside. She handed Maeve a small flashlight. "Don't turn on the lights. We don't want anyone to see."

Maeve wasted no time shining the narrow beam toward the stairs. Nothing lurked there, but her heart hammered against her ribs. The heat didn't help. Someone had turned off the swamp cooler when Phyllis's body was removed, and the sun had been beating on the building for days. A sudden claustrophobic need to get out of the house gripped Maeve. She edged for the door, colliding with Tara.

"Wrong way," Tara said, shoving Maeve toward the living room.

Maeve wanted to argue, but arguing with Tara never did much good. Instead, she marched forward, asking, "What are we doing here?"

"Just putting something right before we go," Tara said. "Now shh. We don't want anyone to hear us."

They moved from the kitchen to the living room, and Maeve's stomach turned. Whether her eyes were open or closed, she saw Phyllis's dead body on the floor. Someone had cleaned up the presents, and she knew Phyllis was deep in the ground, but her mind put the old woman back on the braided rug, staring at the grandfather clock as the abstract faces in the decorative flourishes stared back.

The clock chimed loudly, startling Maeve back into the present. It played the old, familiar song that all clocks seem to know, but the notes sounded off—flat and melancholy. Maeve shuddered, anticipating the eleven tones that would mark the hour.

Bong...

Then... nothing.

Silence fell. Maeve stared at the clock's face, her brow furrowed in puzzlement. She shone her flashlight on her wristwatch. Eleven p.m. But the clock appeared to be out of time as well as tune, with the crooked hour hand pointed stubbornly at the one.

She frowned. Hadn't it been stuck at two o'clock during the party? And she'd sat in this house for half the day; the clock had never once chimed the hour.

"Maeve!" Tara jerked her roughly by the arm. "Keep up!"

"Sorry," Maeve whispered.

She allowed herself to be led up the creaking stairs to the second floor. The ceiling was lower here than in the rooms below and the temperature several degrees warmer. Maeve wished she had something cold to drink but wasn't about to go back to the kitchen by herself to get one.

"Come on," Tara said. "Let's check her bedroom first."

"Check it for what?"

"You know what a coffee can looks like, right? Or did your dad stop drinking that too?"

A red tub of Folgers was an ever-present fixture on the counter at home. Maeve nodded.

"It'll be a metal one, not the plastic ones like they have now. Round and about this high." Tara held her hands apart for reference. "Look everywhere. Under the bed, in the drawers—*everywhere*."

"But why?" Maeve asked as she rummaged through the bedside drawer. "Can't you just get coffee at the gas station?"

Tara stood on her tiptoes and shone her flashlight across the shelf in Phyllis's closet. "There hasn't been coffee in that can for seventy years, kiddo. It's full of money now."

Maeve stopped sifting through the pill bottles and stared up at Tara with wide, confused eyes. "But... isn't that stealing?"

"What?" Tara glanced back at her daughter. Seeing Maeve's

conflicted expression, she smiled and sat on the edge of the bed. When Maeve didn't move, she patted the comforter.

Maeve lowered herself onto the bed cautiously. Tara's posture reminded her of the day her stepmom had explained puberty. That had been awkward enough; she didn't want to sit through it all over again with a woman she barely knew.

"Did you know I grew up here?" Tara asked. "Just three streets away. I'll show you when we leave, drive you by my parents' old house. They're both gone, you know."

Maeve nodded. She still had two sets of grandparents, but she knew only one of them was really related to her.

"Aunt Phyllis never had kids of her own, and my parents weren't around much, even when they were around. So I used to drop by this house every Friday on my way home from school. We'd get out early on Fridays, and Phyllis liked it when I'd visit." A wistful smile crossed Tara's face. "We'd sit on the back patio, and she'd tell me stories, and every week, she'd give me a five-dollar bill. That was a lot of money in those days."

"Sounds nice."

"She was," Tara said quietly. Then she grinned. "Paranoid, though. She always told me, 'Never put your money in banks, Tara. You don't know what they're doing with it.' I figured out pretty quick that all those five-dollar bills weren't coming from Wells Fargo. Around here, old folks like Phyllis use coffee cans to store anything important. Somewhere in this house, there's a can with thousands of dollars—maybe *tens* of thousands, who knows."

"But that money doesn't belong to us," Maeve said in a small voice.

Tara's eyes hardened. "Well, it should, dammit! Phyllis died intestate. I heard it at the funeral. Everything's going to Uncle Hank, and let me tell you, he's a real piece of work. That old shit lives two streets away and never bothered to visit his sister. I'm the only one who ever did. If Phyllis had made a will, I know she'd want me to have the money."

Maeve was silent. She didn't agree with Tara's logic, but she didn't know how to tell her so.

Downstairs, the grandfather clock chimed the quarter hour, playing four quick, descending notes. Somehow, despite the walls and floor that separated Phyllis's bedroom from the clock, the sound was louder than before. Maeve shivered and tightened her grip on the shaking flashlight in her hands.

"Shit, we've been here too long." Tara regarded her daughter with a weary expression. "Look, you're too young to understand. Just help Mommy find the coffee can, okay? The sooner we find it, the sooner we can go home."

That was something Maeve could agree with. She hopped off the bed and set to work, following Tara around the room and looking in cupboards, drawers, and other low spaces. They tackled the upstairs bathroom next and were combing through the tiny guest bedroom when Maeve felt it—the little prickle at the back of her neck that meant someone was watching her.

She whipped her head around and shone her flashlight toward the door. Nobody was there. But as she pulled the beam away, she blinked, and in the instant before her eyelids connected, she swore the outline of a man filled the doorway.

With one hand over her mouth, she backed into Tara and tugged at her sleeve. "Mom," she whispered. "There's someone here."

Tara looked up from the steamer trunk she'd been rooting through, eyes bright and alert. She cocked her head and watched the door for a few moments. "I don't hear anything."

"But there could be someone here," Maeve insisted. "Someone quiet. What if one of your cousins is here, looking for the money? What if they—" The sentence clogged in her throat as she struggled to put her deepest fears into words.

Tara sighed. "You're just like your father. How can you stand being so stressed all the time? I told you, I'm the only one who ever visited Phyllis. Nobody else knows about her stash, and nobody else is here. Everything's fine."

Maeve's mind hopped smoothly from visions of greedy, bloodthirsty relatives to images of the evil, glasses-hating demon her cousins had teased her about. What if they weren't joking—or only thought they were?

"It could be that thing," she whispered. "The thing that's killing everyone."

"Dammit, Maeve. I don't have time for your theatrics right now." Tara gave her daughter a firm shove toward the door. "Come on."

Having finished the upper floor, they circled back down to the living room. The instant Maeve's feet touched the braided rug, the clock chimed again. The eight notes marking the half hour boomed, shaking the windows and rattling Maeve's bones. She clapped her hands over her ears and cried out in alarm.

Tara swatted the back of Maeve's head, knocking her ponytail loose. "Quit being so dramatic."

Her head stung, and Maeve blinked back tears. The room swam briefly before her eyes, but not before she saw the way the shadows moved around the clock. The darkness fluttered like gossamer curtains in front of an open window, and Maeve was sure she saw the silhouette of a stooped old woman slip out of the clock's closed cabinet.

"Let's check the cellar," Tara decided. "She's probably got it down there with all her preserves."

Maeve clutched the back of Tara's T-shirt as they crept through the kitchen and down the creaking staircase. The damp scent of mildew tickled her nose, and she sneezed several times while half-heartedly pawing through the rotted cardboard boxes crowding the dirt floor.

Tara focused on searching the wooden shelves lining the walls. Glass jars clinked as she shoved them around, and she muttered a steady stream of profanity under her breath. Maeve recognized the signs of Tara's impatience; these words were the same that flowed from her mother's mouth if Maeve's father was slow to get his checkbook at the end of their "mommy-daughter" afternoons.

As she worked, Maeve kept one eye fixed on the steps, frequently raising her flashlight from the boxes to make sure nothing had followed them downstairs. Her progress was slow, and Tara barked at her to pick up the pace.

When the grandfather clock struck again, the sound seemed to come from directly above them, rumbling through the floorboards and sending clouds of dust through Maeve's flashlight beam. The song was longer than it'd been at the half hour, but it cut off without resolving, leaving her feeling strangely unbalanced.

The light trembled in her hands. Footsteps creaked above, each one sending another sprinkling of dust onto Maeve's head.

"Mom," she whispered. "There's somebody up there."

"We've been through this, sweetie." Tara didn't bother turning around. "There's nobody here but us."

"But—"

Tara lowered her hands from the shelves and curled them into fists at her sides. Her voice was steady, but her words were clipped. "No buts. Just keep looking."

Maeve fell silent, but she couldn't tear her eyes or the beam of her flashlight off the ceiling above. She waited, barely breathing, and strained her ears for the sound of another footfall.

After a while, Tara seemed to notice the silence in the room. She sighed and squeezed her temples with one hand. "If I'd known you'd be this useless, I would never have brought you here."

"I wish you hadn't," Maeve wailed. Fear overcame her, and tears streamed down her face. "I don't want to be here anymore. Please, please let me go. I just want to go home."

"For God's sake, keep your voice down!" Tara hissed. "What is wrong with you? You're too old to be afraid of the dark."

"It's not just the dark." Maeve stared up at the ceiling, her lower lip trembling. "It's the clock. There's something wrong with it, something evil."

"The clock!" Tara slapped herself lightly on the forehead. "That old bat probably moved the can into the clock—that's what she was doing when she died, hiding it in the little cupboard!"

Without waiting for her daughter, Tara ran up the stairs, taking them two at a time. Maeve scrambled after her but was still only in the kitchen when she heard Tara's shout of triumph from the living room.

"Maeve, you're a genius!" Tara called. "We're—"

Tara's next word was cut off by the clanging of the grandfather clock. It played the full tune this time, and each of the sixteen notes sent a shock of ice through Maeve's veins. She froze and held her breath as she waited for the clock to toll the hour.

She barely heard the single, incorrect *bong*. Tara's scream, infinitely louder and more terrified than it had been the day she found Phyllis's body, rattled Maeve's skull and drowned out every other sound.

Maeve wanted to run forward, to round the corner into the living room and save her mother. But her feet carried her backward, and she tumbled out the kitchen door and down the steps to the patio. Her breath rushed back into her lungs, and she cried out for help, screaming as loudly as she could.

Lights flicked on in the surrounding houses. Maeve curled into a ball on the ground, sobbing into her hands as the clock finally finished chiming the time with eleven more long, dull *bongs*.

By the time the paramedics arrived, Tara was long past saving. Her dead eyes were frozen on the clock's face, locked on the crooked little hour hand that now pointed stoutly upward toward the twelve.

WATCHERS' WARNING

Three cats watched us from the house beyond the stop sign. They met my eyes, blinking in near unison behind the window glass as Fiona brought the car to a halt, then turned away in disinterest before we pulled into the intersection.

"Look how far apart the houses are, Ripley," Fiona said. "I've never lived somewhere this rural before."

Neither had I. I shared her sense of wonder at all the space around us. Stretches of land as long as two or three city blocks separated each home from the next. Miles beyond the road on either side, rugged mountains stretched toward the sky. Closer to the highway, sagging fence lines kept herds of livestock corralled in place.

My tail twitched. The cows made me nervous, but the smaller sheep looked fun to chase around.

Fiona laughed. "You're adorable. If I weren't driving, I'd get a picture of you with your paws up on the window like that."

I didn't respond. I'd long since learned humans couldn't understand Cat, but I absorbed the compliment, pleased she recognized my charisma. She had a bit of her own, with her dark curls and bright green eyes. Most enticingly, she wore a lavender perfume that made me want to chew on her sweatshirt.

It had been a long drive. I'd never been in a car for so many hours in a row. It had only taken a few minutes to get from the shelter to my last family's house, and the return ride back in the animal control van had been far too short.

All the way up here, Fiona chattered away, filling me in on her life story. And the more she talked, the more nervous I became.

Her life was frighteningly volatile. She moved around constantly, always looking for a fresh start. We hadn't gotten to her new house yet, and she already wondered aloud if we'd still be there six months from now or if we'd move somewhere warmer for the winter.

Being in a warm place sounded nice. I shivered, remembering the winter I'd been a Christmas gift from a man to his girlfriend. They'd fed me tuna juice right from the can, then broke up just after New Year's. Neither one wanted to keep me. I spent the next several months living outside, sleeping under cars, and scrounging for scraps in dumpsters until animal control picked me up.

Fiona hummed as we passed a tall farmhouse. A half dozen cats lounged on the covered porch, and still more watched us from the second-floor windows. I wondered if I would be an outside cat.

I hoped not. I'd had enough of the outdoors.

At last, we turned down a long gravel driveway crowded by trees on either side. Fiona drove slowly through the curves, wincing as stray branches scraped the sides of her station wagon. I didn't know why she minded; the car was old and already beat up. After a few minutes, the pines opened up, and the house came into view—a single-story wooden building painted a faded blue.

"Thank goodness." Fiona stretched her arms above her head. "I hope there's toilet paper in there."

Despite my efforts to make myself as limp and unmanageable

as possible, she wrestled me back into the cardboard carrier she'd gotten at the shelter. I yowled my displeasure, and she lifted the carrier up to her face until one of her eyes appeared through an air hole.

"Calm your paws. It's only for a minute."

It was more than a minute. She left me in the carrier while she used the bathroom *and* while she brought in her suitcases and boxes. My tail thrashed against the cardboard. Didn't she understand we couldn't settle here until I had a chance to investigate?

She was only human. Her nose wasn't up to the job of making sure we were safe or sniffing out pests infesting the walls. As I started clawing at one of the air holes, she let me out.

I stretched my front legs, digging into the rug. The threadbare material was worthless for sharpening my claws. I eyed the faded green-and-white striped couch. Upholstery was usually—

"Don't even think about it." Fiona knelt next to me and unwrapped a scratching pad. "I'm not supposed to have pets here. If you scratch the furniture, the jig'll be up."

I exercised my claws on the pad for a few moments, working out my stiff muscles after the long car ride. Then, not one to be left behind, I followed Fiona as she explored our new home.

The layout reminded me of the fourth house I'd lived in. The front door opened into a small furnished living room. Across from the couch, a tall bookcase stood next to a boxy TV that looked older than anything I'd seen before. Overall, it smelled okay. No mold or rot or mouse droppings. Just dust, with the barest hint of something else that I couldn't put my paw on.

Through a doorway, yellow cupboards filled the small kitchen. Like every house I'd lived in, a Watcher sat in a corner of the ceiling. Its black shape expanded and contracted, and its six eyes rolled lazily in multiple directions. I stared at it for a while in case it wanted to stare back. It didn't seem interested, not even when

Fiona entered the room and searched the shelves for food.

"Crap," she said. "I forgot to stop at the grocery store. I'll run out in a few. Come on—let's put your litter box in the cellar."

Between the kitchen and the bathroom, a narrow door provided access to a flight of wooden steps. They creaked under Fiona's weight, and I was on the verge of following her down when the thick, sour stench of rotten flesh hit my nose.

This was the smell I'd gotten a whiff of in the living room, and I realized now that the odor must have wafted up through the floorboards. Something lurked down there, something rancid. The sharp tang warned me that whatever it was, it wasn't safe to eat.

"Come on, Ripley," Fiona called. "Here kitty, kitty."

How could she stand to be down there? Even at the top of the stairs, the smell was overpowering. I wouldn't be able to breathe at the bottom.

She furrowed her brow at me when she came back up. I sniffed her shoes. The putrid stench covered them. I swept back my whiskers and bared my fangs, my mouth open in the universal Cat sign for "This is a stinky thing." But instead of taking off her sneakers and burning them in a fire, she bent down and scooped me up.

"No!" I yowled, trying to squirm out of her grasp. "I don't want to go down there!"

Like in the car, she somehow outwitted and overpowered me. Before I could escape her clutches, we were in the basement. She dropped me into the litter box, and I spun around to glare at her in a shower of gray particles.

"You're potty-trained, right?" she said. "This is where you can do your business."

I looked past her, plotting my escape. The room was small, about the size of the kitchen. In front of bare stone walls, deep wooden shelves ran the length of the space. Boxes of ancient vegetables filled them, but they weren't the source of the smell.

Unlike the wooden floors above, the floor here was hard-packed earth, no different from the empty lots back in the city. The decomposing thing responsible for that awful odor was buried somewhere down here; I sensed it. Oddest of all, two more Watchers hung from the ceiling. Only once before had I seen more than one of them in the same room, and it wasn't a memory I wanted to revisit.

Why were there so many Watchers here?

My natural catly need to know the answer to every question was no match for the fear that ran up my back at the sight of multiple Watchers. Each hair along my tail and spine puffed outward, and I shot out of the litter box, reaching the stairs in a single bound and the main floor two leaps after that. I bolted into the living room to clean my paws of the offending stench and glared at the open door to the cellar. If Fiona didn't put the litter box somewhere less horrifying, the mess would be in her shoes.

LUCKILY FOR BOTH OF US, Fiona got the message. She moved the box into a space between the bathtub and the toilet, telling me it made more sense if we both used the bathroom for the same purpose. I rewarded her for understanding by chasing a feathered stick she dragged back and forth across the living room rug for me.

I wanted to like her. At the shelter, she'd purchased two cases of pâté, a large bag of catnip, the cardboard scratcher, and a pile of toys. She seemed committed to keeping me around... but so had my last several humans.

Right until they weren't.

As we played, the Watcher from the kitchen oozed its way along the ceiling and took up residence in the corner of the living room above the front door. A few minutes later, the doorbell rang.

Fiona stood on her toes to look through the peephole before whipping around to stare at me. I knew that face; she'd made the same expression in the hallway, right before she grabbed me. I tensed, and as she moved toward me, I bolted left, jumped on top of the TV set, and from there, evaded her grasp by leaping up to the top of the tall bookcase. There was exactly enough room for me to hunker down beneath the ceiling, well out of her reach.

"Ripley, come down from there!" she ordered in a loud whisper.

I hunched forward, flattening myself against the bookcase. The doorbell sounded again.

Fiona pursed her lips as the doorbell rang again. "Okay, stay up there and don't make a sound," she said and opened the door.

"Hello!" a high-pitched woman's voice drifted in from the porch. "You must be Fiona!"

"Um, yes." Fiona smoothed her sweatshirt. "And you are?"

"Agnes Priest, from Guardian. We spoke on the phone."

Without waiting for an invitation, Agnes pushed her way past Fiona and stepped into the living room. She was a petite woman—Fiona towered over her—but she moved with confidence. All six of the Watcher's eyes followed Agnes as she placed a large plastic-covered basket on the coffee table and spun around to offer Fiona her hand.

"On behalf of the entire Guardian team, I'd like to welcome you to town!" She beamed up at Fiona. "We're so excited to have you on board."

"Um, thanks. Would you like to sit down?"

Agnes waved dismissively. "Oh, no. I can't stay. I just wanted to drop by and make sure you're all set for Monday."

Fiona's shoulders relaxed. "I think so, apart from finding the nearest grocery store."

"There's a supermarket about fifteen miles down the highway, but I'm sure this will tide you over for tonight." Agnes flicked the bow atop the gift basket. "Well, I've got a hungry family waiting for me at home, so I'll get out of your hair and let you settle in."

As she turned to leave, the toe of her shoe caught the feathered stick Fiona had been teasing me with earlier. Agnes bent at the waist, picked up the toy, and frowned at Fiona. "You don't have a cat, do you?"

"Not anymore," Fiona lied smoothly. "The lease doesn't allow pets, right? So I gave my cat to my sister. That's just a memento."

My whiskers twitched. She'd told me on the way here that she didn't have any family left, which made it easier to move around from place to place.

"Yes, Guardian Corporation has a strict no-pet policy in all of its rental units," said Agnes, rolling the stick between her fingers before handing it back to Fiona. "I'm sorry you had to say goodbye to your cat. It's nice you have a keepsake. Good night."

As quickly as she'd pushed her way inside, Agnes slipped out the door. The instant the latch *snicked* into place behind her, the Watcher's six eyes lolled back into their undirected, unfocused state.

I shivered. Normally, Watchers didn't bother me. They're everywhere, as ubiquitous and harmless as daddy longlegs in the garden. There's one in every house, but humans never notice them, and Watchers don't seem to notice humans. Yet here, in this remote place, there were three. Why? The living room Watcher's eyes had followed Agnes, exactly as another Watcher's gaze followed my cage-mate, Tiger, into the Bad Room at the shelter— the room that swallowed up any cat who lingered there too long.

Forcing the memory from my mind, I gave myself a good shake and leaped from the bookcase to rub against Fiona's shins. I could tell the visit left her feeling stressed. She scratched me along my spine as she sat on the couch. After indulging her need to love on me, I hopped onto the coffee table and sniffed Agnes's welcome gift.

"Well, let's see what we've got." Fiona pulled the bow off the basket and started emptying it of bottles and cans.

The coffee table was soon full of food. The last item in the collection was a small smooth stone about the size of a mouse. The light from the fixture above us reflected off its shiny black surface, and Fiona turned it over between her hands.

"Weird," she muttered. She set the stone down to examine the food.

None of the cans or jars had pictures of fish on them, and they were too tightly sealed for me to tell what was inside. Still, I sniffed at them, hoping to catch a whiff of tuna or sardines.

"Oh, yum." Fiona held up a jar filled with a yellow substance. "Cheese dip! But…. Hmm. That's odd."

I tilted my head in question. Fiona snorted and showed me the label.

"It's expired." She rifled through the rest of the goods. "All of them are expired by, like, two years. What kind of cheap company sends an expired welcome gift?"

She tossed the food into the basket, stood up, and grabbed her purse. "Well, no choice now. I have to hit that grocery store. Be good. I'll be back soon."

I'D NEARLY FINISHED sniffing my way around the baseboards in the kitchen when the front doorknob rattled a few hours later. Hoping Fiona had returned with something containing tuna, I hustled into the living room to sniff at the crack beneath the door.

I skidded to a stop halfway across the rug. All three Watchers had congregated above the front door, their shadowy forms undulating in rhythm with one another. Their eighteen collective eyes were locked on to the doorknob, which rotated slowly from left to right and back again.

Even at a distance of several feet, I could smell the thick ropes of noxious fumes that crept through the crack beneath the door. The odor reminded me of an amplified version of too-old fish. The sickening stench overpowered my senses in an instant, and the fur on my neck rose. I shot across the room and onto the TV set. The knob rattled again, just as I made it up to my hiding spot atop the bookcase.

The door creaked open.

It wasn't Fiona.

The figure in the doorway stood two heads taller than she did, and he scraped the sides of the frame as he stepped through. His body looked similar to that of a human male, but this man-*thing* lacked any facial features and wore no clothes. His gait was slow and lumbering, and his trunk-like feet left soggy footprints on the hardwood floor as he lurched toward the coffee table.

The many eyes of each Watcher stalked his steps.

I flattened myself against the top of the bookcase. My ears swept backward, and apart from an uncontrollable tremble in my whiskers, I held as still as possible. Everything about this creature screamed *danger*!

The wet figure moaned as he leaned over the coffee table and picked up the odd black stone from the gift basket with a swollen hand. He brought it to his featureless face, which split horizontally and formed a dripping maw. The stone disappeared inside, and his skin oozed back together, erasing any evidence of where his mouth had been. With a thundering moan that rattled the bookcase against the wall, the beast made for the kitchen.

As the thing passed me, I suppressed a shudder, wishing I could retract my whiskers into my face to make myself even smaller. His lack of eyes unnerved me. There was no way to know if he saw me. I'd just have to be ready to hurtle past him if he reached for me.

Meanwhile, the Watchers had more than enough eyes between them. They slouched along the ceiling and followed the intruder into the hallway. The temptation to join their parade was strong, especially when I heard the stairs to the cellar creak beneath the thing's weight. What was it looking for? Was it searching for the source of that terrible smell? Was the stink in the cellar its food or its mate?

I crept forward to the edge of the bookcase and teetered there. I was very small…. Surely it wouldn't notice me if I sneaked—

The staircase creaked again, and I shook myself. Stupid, stupid. I wasn't some kitten, prone to mischief and getting myself into trouble. I was old enough, wise enough, and experienced enough to be cautious. But despite the thing's soggy flesh and corrupt odor, it possessed an undeniable draw.

Back in the hallway, the beast roared like a predator who couldn't reach its prey. I shrank back and watched as it trudged across the living room and onto the porch. The door swung closed behind it, the latch pointlessly *snicking* into place.

"RIPLEY! I'M HOME," Fiona's voice called.

Suspecting a trick, I stayed in the warm space beneath the bed. What if that thing had come back and could mimic her sound? My heart pounded against my rib cage at the soft thump of footsteps moving down the short hallway.

A moment later, Fiona's large eyes peered at me from the foot of the bed.

"What are you doing under there, silly?" She produced a bag of tuna crunchies and shook it. "Look what I got you at the store."

The telltale scent of fish and the faint aroma of her lavender perfume were powerful enough to lure me out from my hiding place. Fiona scattered a few treats on the floor and flounced onto the mattress with a deep sigh.

"This place is nuts," she told me as I gobbled up my snack. "It took forever to get to the store, and everyone there looked at me like I was an alien. Seriously, how hard is it to smile back at someone? And then I thought I should drive to the Guardian office so I'll know how long it will take me to get to work Monday, but I couldn't find it. I must've written the address down wrong because the building number I have doesn't exist. I drove around for over an hour searching for it. I'll call Agnes tomorrow."

When the treats were gone, I jumped onto the bed to sniff her. She scratched the top of my head, and I nuzzled her hand.

"We have to leave," I meowed. "It's not safe here."

Fiona laughed. "Look at you, so demanding! You can have all the petting you want as soon as I shower."

I stood in the bathroom doorway, checking the hall for danger as Fiona bathed. My ears were on high alert, twitching toward every tiny sound. There were no mice in the walls. No birds in the trees outside. Just a low wind tugging on the siding.

After her shower, Fiona turned in for the night, falling asleep too easily in the new bed in this strange house. How do humans acclimate so quickly, especially in a situation that is obviously dangerous?

They're too trusting. Too naive.

My whiskers quivered as I watched her sleep. We would find no safety here. Tomorrow, I had to convince her to leave this house behind.

"RIPLEY, WERE YOU CHEWING THESE?" Fiona smiled down at me the next day, holding a pair of white socks in one hand and resting her other fist on her hip. "I found them by the front door, along with my sneakers."

"Put them on!" I meowed sharply. "Let's go!"

She bent down and ruffled the fur on my back. "All these toys, and you want to play with my socks. Cats are peculiar."

Humming, she unpacked her suitcases and boxes. I glared at

her, frustrated that she didn't understand. What did I have to do, drag her to the car?

I huffed. If only it were that easy. Humans were too heavy and too stubborn. I needed to get my message across some other way.

In the meantime, I kept an eye on the Watcher in the kitchen. Why the two who had come up from the cellar went back downstairs, I didn't know, but I couldn't stomach facing that stench again to find out.

When Fiona took a break from unpacking for lunch, she pulled her cell phone out of her purse and entered a number.

"Hello, Agnes," she said after a moment. "This is Fiona."

My ears fluttered. I could hear Agnes's voice in reply. "Fiona! Uh... well. This is a surprise."

"I'm sorry to bother you on a Sunday, but I wondered if you could confirm the address of our office. I must've written it down wrong, because I couldn't find it last night."

"Ah... um, yes. Hold on one moment."

Fiona raised an eyebrow at me. I crept closer to the phone. Yesterday, Agnes had spoken with speed and confidence. Why was she acting so oddly today?

"Here we are." Agnes coughed. "Excuse me. It's... uh, 1954 Carlson Road."

"So strange," said Fiona. "I thought I was right there, but I didn't see it. I'm a little worried about finding it tomorrow."

"Oh, you're not the first person to get lost in a new town." Agnes's voice was growing stronger, and she sounded more like she had the day before. "I'll tell you what—I'll pick you up in the morning, and we'll drive there together."

Fiona sagged against the couch cushions and smiled. "That'd be great. Thank you."

"My pleasure. Say, did I happen to leave a black stone in your welcome basket?"

The skin along my back rippled. The intruder had picked up that rock and ingested it. It was the first thing he did. If Agnes knew about the stone... if she was asking about it....

My whiskers bristled.

She knew about the creature.

"A black rock? I think so." Fiona leaned forward again and rummaged through the contents of the basket. "I could have sworn it was here yesterday, but I'm not seeing it now."

"Don't worry about it. It's not valuable. I just wondered where it'd gone. I'll see you in the morning then. Goodbye."

"Wait, Agnes," Fiona called. "What time will you be here?"

"Oh, right. Let's say eight o'clock, shall we?"

"That sounds—hello? Agnes?" Fiona pulled the phone away from her face and frowned, then turned to me with raised eyebrows. "She hung up on me. What a weird woman. Should I tell her all that food was expired?"

"You should tell her not to bother picking you up tomorrow," I said. "Because we'll be far away from here."

"Nah, I won't say anything. I don't want to embarrass her."

Fiona stood and surveyed the living room. She had arranged her collection of books on the shelves, and the cardboard boxes she'd brought into the house were empty. On a normal day, I'd have liked to play in those boxes. One was small enough to squeeze into. But today, I was a cat on a mission. I had to convince Fiona to get out of here before the stinky creature returned.

"I think I'll take a nap," she told me. "This country air makes me sleepy."

I followed her into the bedroom. She settled on the bed and pulled the covers up around her, yawning. It was unacceptable. This wasn't the time for sleep! We needed to leave.

I jumped onto her face.

"Ouch!" she shouted, shoving me to the floor. "You scratched my nose!"

She rolled over with her back to me. I narrowed my eyes. There was one sound I knew from experience would wake any human, no matter the depth of their slumber. I hopped back on the bed, hunched my shoulders, and started working a hair ball out of my throat.

Three coughs in, Fiona leaped to her feet.

Victory! I thought.

It was short lived. She grabbed me around my middle and dropped me into the hall.

"Alright, kiddo," she said. "Your bedroom privileges are officially revoked."

With that, she closed the door, leaving me to fume in the hallway by myself. I stalked to the kitchen, planning to annoy her out of bed by tugging on the cupboard doors so they clunked against the wood again and again, but I realized that would be pointless. She wouldn't connect that to a need to leave; she would just think I was being obnoxious. She might even get so irritated that she'd take me back to the shelter… and I was out of time there.

I gulped. There was only one thing to do. I had to prove to Fiona that something was terribly wrong in this house.

MY HAIR STOOD OUT in all directions. My tail swelled, and every instinct in my body screamed at me to run away from the sickly sweet stench that filled the cellar, but I was resolute. Forcing myself not to think about how long it would take me to get this smell out of my fur, I started digging.

The ground at the bottom of the stairs was cold and hard beneath my paws. Above me, the pair of Watchers clung to the ceiling, their eyes rolling listlessly. They puffed and receded, growing and shrinking as I scratched ineffectively at the packed dirt at the foot of the stairs.

After a few minutes, I stopped and glared around the cellar. The room was small, but time was short. Who knew when that thing would come back? It had been dark when it showed up the night before. Did I only have until nightfall to get Fiona out of the house?

Much as it pained my nose to do so, I sniffed along the floor, hoping to catch an even stronger scent—if that was possible. The foul odor had permeated everything in the room, and I gagged as I searched. At last, the stench intensified beneath one of the long shelves against the back wall. I began digging. The dirt there was looser and more cooperative than it was by the stairs. It came away easily, like litter in a box.

The farther down I delved, the stronger the smell became. It was the scent of death, something I was all too familiar with from winters spent outside and too many trips to the shelter.

Just over a foot down, I found it: a decomposing human hand.

The odor exploded around me as I pulled it free of the dirt. It was still attached to a buried arm, and I could only move it far enough into the room that the shelf no longer shielded it from view.

I bolted back to the stairs and yowled, calling to Fiona in my loudest and most urgent voice. "Fiooooona!" I howled. "Come seeeeeee!"

The Watchers were disinterested in my song. Their eyes were fixed on the hand, now clearly visible from my spot on the bottom step.

It took several long minutes of continuous yowling before Fiona's footsteps sounded in the hallway above.

"Ripley!" she called, poking her head through the doorway. "What are you doing, warming up for American Idol?"

She jogged lightly down the stairs, stopping short just four steps from the dirt floor. Her face paled, and she covered her nose with the end of her sweatshirt. "What in God's name is that smell?"

"Here!" I meowed, dashing over to the unearthed prize. "Look!"

Fiona followed, squinting in the dim light and breathing shallowly. When she saw the hand, she screamed, scooped me up, and pounded back up the steps and into her bedroom. "What the hell," she shouted, digging in her bag for her cell phone. "What the *hell*!"

Fumbling and perspiring, she dialed the phone. I heard a man's voice on the other end.

"Sheriff's office. What is your emergency?"

"My name is Fiona Adams. I just found a body buried in my basement!"

"Fiona Adams, you say? New gal at Guardian?"

"Yes." She nestled the phone between her shoulder and her ear, leaving her hands free to pull a suitcase out of her closet.

"I know where you are, ma'am. Stay put. I'll have a deputy out to you ASAP."

"Thank you. I—" Fiona stared at her phone with wide eyes, then threw it onto the bed. "He hung up on me!"

I watched her throw a few clothes into the suitcase before she snatched me up in her free arm. "No way am I staying in here. We're going to a motel."

Not bothering with a carrier, she marched into the living room.

The two Watchers from the cellar had joined the one above the front door, and their eyes were all focused on Fiona. I hissed and struggled to get out of her grasp.

"I smell danger!" I howled.

As usual, she didn't understand. She yanked the door open,

recoiling as a wet, rotten stink slammed into us with brute force.

The creature waited on the porch.

One arm was outstretched toward us as though he'd been about to turn the knob and let himself in. Eyeless, mouthless, soulless, the thing lurched forward, reaching for Fiona.

She dropped me. I bolted backward, once more leaping to safety atop the bookcase.

"Run!" I hissed from my perch.

She should have easily been able to outrun it. I screamed at her to move, but she simply stood there, mouth hanging open and arms frozen in a defensive posture in front of her face.

The creature moved inside. With a swing of his hand, he knocked Fiona to the floor.

The Watchers leered, their many eyes bulging from the inky voids that formed their bodies.

"Help her!" I shouted.

They didn't intervene. They just watched, earning their name and nothing more, as Fiona lay there, motionless.

The intruder crouched over her like a feral cat over its prey. Its face split in two. In a series of rough jerks, the black stone reemerged as though it were being regurgitated. Cloudy fluid dripped from the stone's shining surface as the creature dragged his stone tongue across Fiona's cheek.

She didn't blink. I don't know if she couldn't or if she didn't dare to look away. Her mouth was frozen in the open shape of a soundless scream.

He was going to eat her. Fiona, who was strong enough to never stop looking for happiness and bighearted enough to want company on her journey. Fiona, who adopted me just in time to keep me from going into the Bad Room from which no cats returned.

Sure, her instincts were terrible. Sure, she didn't understand a word I said. But she was mine now. Mine. And he was going to just barge in and devour *my* Person?

Not on my watch.

"Get away from her!" I shrieked, hurling myself off the shelf.

The thing yanked his head up, and two sunken eyes took shape above his mouth. They widened in shock as I flew across the room. A deep-rooted moan shook the house.

I slammed squarely into his chest with all four paws, claws out and slashing. Steam poured from the gashes I made in his oozing skin. He seemed to shrink, and he roared in anger. The black rock dropped from his mouth and clunked against the floor.

Fiona gasped, then screamed. She kicked at the creature as I scratched and tore at his flesh with my fangs. I smelled nothing. I tasted nothing. I was pure instinct and adrenaline, defending her with every ounce of strength I could muster.

I dropped to the floor as the thing stumbled backward. He tumbled off the porch and collapsed into the flower bed. As soon as he cleared the open doorway, the Watchers' eyes closed briefly. A moment later, they opened again, each looking in a different direction.

The message was clear: we were safe, for the moment. But moments have a habit of passing quickly.

Fiona wasted no time collecting her purse in one arm and me in the other. My heart beat against my chest as we fled to the safety of the station wagon. Within seconds, she started the engine, swung around in a wide arc, and sped back along the driveway. Just before we reached the highway, we passed a police car pulled halfway off the road, its lights dark and siren silent. Fiona's headlights illuminated the interior of the cruiser, and a young man glared out at us with narrowed eyes.

"Don't stop," I warned her.

She hunched over the steering wheel and gunned the engine, powering to the end of the driveway and screeching onto the highway without slowing. We drove in silence for the better part of an hour before Fiona relaxed against her seat and stretched her arms. She reached out and scratched me behind my left ear.

"You saved my life," she told me.

I nuzzled her hand. "Call us even."

UNTIL DEATH

"Get up," Paige whispered, voice cracking. A sob escaped her throat as she shook Adam's shoulders, but nothing she did could wake him.

She closed her eyes and raked her hands through her thin hair, rocking on the edge of the mattress as she chanted, "Please, please get up!" But when she opened them again, nothing had changed. This wasn't the kind of nightmare she could leave behind come morning. This was the living kind, and one she'd been dreading for months.

Time hadn't prepared her the way she'd hoped it would, the way the doctors and the parish priest had claimed it could. Who would feel ready for death to visit their own bed?

"This isn't how it's supposed to happen!" she shouted at her husband. "We're supposed to be together, forever and for always, remember?"

Adam didn't stir.

"That's why we made them change our vows." She clawed her nails down her hollow cheekbones. "'Until death' wasn't for us."

The last word faded into a sorrowful wail as Paige collapsed onto her husband. Her body trembled, shaking free the tears that welled up in her eyes, and she doubted she would ever stop shivering.

Seconds grew into minutes, which stretched into hours, and at last Paige knew what had to happen. Fate might not have chosen to take them together, but that didn't mean they would have to be apart for long. Her mind drifted to the sleeping pills in the medicine cabinet and Adam's straight razor on the bathroom sink, but another idea struck her, one that wouldn't require her to leave his side even for a moment.

Resting one hand on his chest and the other on her own, she leaned down to kiss him for the last time.

Her lips lingered on his. No air moved between them. No breaths snuck in or out.

Then his heartbeat slowed beneath her fingertips.

Slowed…

Slowed…

And stopped.

Paige's tears stopped flowing. Adam's chest stopped moving. He rose from the bed, and they surveyed the bodies they'd left behind, hers now hours cold.

Hand in hand, together again, they faded into the next life.

A FRIEND IN NEED

The impossibility exhausted me. She couldn't be there. But in defiance of all logic, Emily lurked in the corner of the classroom, trying to catch my eye from behind Dr. Radcliffe's desk. It took effort to ignore her, to block out the stare that burned into my forehead in a way it had never done while she was still awake. I refused to look, choosing instead to focus on the half-empty can of Super Energy Blast at the edge of my desk.

"She's not here," I muttered to the can. "She's not here."

The repeated mantra didn't do any good. Emily remained, her brown eyes wide and unblinking, same as she'd done for the past week. No matter where I was, no matter what time of day... if I got tired enough, she'd be there. Chugging energy drinks bought me a couple sleepless days and nights of peace, but the caffeine crash loomed right around the corner. The fatigue pressed down on me like a weight—God, I wanted to close my eyes. Close them for a minute and rest...

"Still with us, Annie?"

My eyelids snapped open at the sound of Dr. Radcliffe's voice. She frowned at me from beside the blackboard.

"Sorry." I cleared my throat and stretched in my seat, then

grabbed my pen and tried to copy the chart Dr. Radcliffe had written while I'd been dozing. I welcomed the distraction from Emily's gaze, and I took care to write my notes, including more details than I'd ever done in my four years of college.

"As you can see, the grading is very straightforward. If you get your senior projects in on time, follow the formatting guidelines, and stay on topic, there's no reason you won't pass. See me during my office hours if you have additional questions. Class dismissed."

There was a loud scraping of chairs as the other students in my advisory group packed up their things and left the classroom. I stuffed my notebook into my messenger bag, hoping to sneak out while Dr. Radcliffe erased the board, but when I raised my head, she was already standing at my desk.

"Do you have a minute?" she asked.

"Sure." I tried to make it sound casual, like I had no idea what she wanted to talk to me about, but the spike in my voice betrayed me.

Dr. Radcliffe half sat on the desk across from mine and looked at me for a few silent moments. I ran my hands over my head and straightened my ponytail, hoping I didn't look as disheveled as I felt. I showered at least twice a day in my bid to stay awake, but my old routine of straightening my hair and picking fun, layered outfits had long since fallen to the wayside in favor of hair ties and whatever T-shirt smelled cleanest.

At last she spoke, tilting her head toward my energy drink. "Doesn't seem to be working."

"No, not really."

"Listen, I know you've got a lot of finals to study for. And I can't imagine what you must be going through since Emily…" She trailed off and pursed her lips. "Well, I'm extending the deadline on your senior project. Why don't you take summer semester to wrap it up?"

I shook my head. "You don't need to do that for me. I'm fine."

"I really think you should. It could make—"

"No." The booming volume of my voice surprised me. I lowered it to explain myself. "I appreciate your concern, but I don't want to delay my graduation."

Another semester here would do me in. I couldn't take the stares from my classmates, the pity from my professors. Emily was the one who'd gotten sick, not me. She was the one who wouldn't wake up. But nobody was trying to help her; they all seemed focused on me.

I didn't get it. I wasn't Emily's only roommate. I wasn't even the one who found her and called the paramedics. I wondered if Zuri's professors offered to extend deadlines or waive assignments. Knowing Zuri, probably not.

"I'll have my project to you next week," I said. "Same as everybody else."

I zipped my backpack and stood. I felt Dr. Radcliffe's eyes following me out of the classroom, but I didn't turn around. Her gaze was a hell of a lot easier to ignore than Emily's.

A VICIOUS FUNK greeted me when I opened the door to our apartment. I glanced at the Jenga tower of dishes piled in the sink, thought about washing them, and opted to open a window and air the place out instead. Cleaning was one of many things I'd avoided since the paramedics wheeled Emily away, and Zuri was too busy with Student Council activities to care that I wasn't pulling my weight. That, or maybe she took the same kind of pity on me as everyone else and just wasn't bitching at me about it.

I shoved an empty pizza box off the couch and stretched out across the soft cushions. It was easier to ignore Emily out here than in our bedroom. In there, she stared at me from the hundreds of selfies and group photos we'd taken together over the last four years. Out here, she only stared at me from the corner where Zuri kept her yoga mat.

"Hey, Emily," I told her. "I know you're a figment of my imagination, but I'd still appreciate it if you'd let me squeeze in a nap before chem lab."

She mouthed something in return, but I couldn't hear it. I could never hear it. The words were probably random song lyrics or something else my brain was too worn-out to process in any healthy way. Maybe after graduation, when there was more space in my head, I'd finally figure it out.

A light hum filled my ears. I felt the forceful tug of sleep on my eyelids. My body, impatient for rest—deep, quality rest—tugged me deeper into the cushions. I closed my eyes and hovered briefly on the edge between consciousness and nothingness.

"Annie!"

Emily's voice slapped the buzz of sleepiness from my mind. It had been exactly twenty-eight days since I last heard it. When I opened my eyes, she wasn't skulking in the corner anymore. She knelt beside the couch, eyes frantic and cheeks flushed.

I scrambled to sit up and backed away from her, pulling my knees to my chest and trying to retreat as far back into the cushions as possible. I trained my eyes on the ceiling fan and whispered my mantra, "She's not here. She's not here."

"Annie, I'm here!"

"She's not here. Not here. Not here." I shook my head and pinched my arms and legs. "I'm dreaming. Wake up!"

"Look at me, Nan!"

I hated that nickname. Emily only used it when she was trying to nettle me. Out of sheer reflex, I turned my head and shot her a glare. Her eyes went wide, and words—finally audible after so long—spilled out of her mouth at light speed.

"Listen! You're awake, and I'm here!" She glanced down at her chest, which was translucent enough that I could see the pile of unwashed clothes behind her. "Or I guess part of me is. My body's still in the hospital. But I hate it there, Annie! Please help me come home!"

I stared at her, really looking for the first time in weeks. "Is it really you?"

She tried to grab for my hand, but she passed right through my body. "Yes, it's me. I've been trying to talk to you for days." A tear rolled down her cheek. "I can't believe you can actually hear me."

My brain imitated my car engine in the dead of winter, half starting and then choking out. Again and again I turned the key, trying to process what the hell was going on here. Emily, in our living room, talking to me... But it couldn't be real. She couldn't be real. I'd seen her the day before in her hospital room, tubes and wires coming out of her throat and arms. She'd been skinnier there, thinner than she looked now, with limp, stringy hair and skin the color of ash.

"You're not here," I whispered. "You're in a coma. You're sick—"

"I'm not sick!" She reached for me again, then seemed to remember that she couldn't touch me and dragged her hand down her face instead. "That's why I need to get out of there. The doctors will *never* be able to help me. It's not an infection or a fever."

I'd never seen that desperate look in her eyes before. Even when she'd been stressed or sad, there'd always been a light, a hint of a smile waiting to be coaxed out by a good joke. I never imagined she could look so frightened.

My chest constricted. This wasn't something I imagined either. This was real. Emily—my best friend, my confidante, the person who'd gotten me through every failed test and bad breakup—sat here, translucent, asking for my help.

I straightened up. "Okay. If you're not sick, why are you in a coma?"

"It was a demon."

"A demon?"

Under different circumstances, I would've laughed. On a normal day, Emily might have been rehearsing for an audition or playing a practical joke. But I didn't think Emily would've stalked me like a living ghost for the past week just to prank me, so I had to take anything she told me at face value.

Which means, I realized, *that she's talking about an honest-to-God actual demon.*

I struggled for words. "I don't... I don't know how I can help with that."

Emily's face was still flushed, but now that I'd agreed she was, in fact, somehow visiting me from the confines of her hospital bed, her pupils had grown still, and she looked less like a desperate addict jonesing for her next fix.

"There's a book in my desk," she said. "Get it. The last page has everything you need to know."

"Okay, I'll be right back."

As much as I loved Emily, my self-preservation instincts wouldn't let me stand up, walk by her, and then turn my back to her to go down the hall. Instead, I climbed over the back of the couch, like a weirdo, and shuffled out of the room in reverse, not turning around until I entered our bedroom and closed the door.

As I'd expected, the wall of selfies assaulted me. I froze, staring at them. Emily was everywhere—smiling, laughing, sharing her brilliant light with the world. I didn't want that light to go out forever. I balled my hands into fists and marched across the room, letting hundreds of pairs of brown eyes follow me to Emily's desk. I hadn't touched so much as a pencil on it since she'd gotten sick—no, since she'd been *taken*—but now I rifled through every stack of paper, upended every drawer in search of whatever book she was talking about. The only books I found were textbooks, and the last pages of those were appendixes and glossaries. Nothing in them suggested, "Hey, I can help with this demon problem."

"Dammit!" I banged my fists on the desk, and something landed on my foot—a small brown book that barely filled my hand when I picked it up. I ran my thumb down the empty spine; there was no title, no markings at all. Just smooth, faded leather. I pulled back on the pages and let them flip past me. Neat, cramped handwriting filled each page.

"A journal," I muttered.

I knew it wasn't Emily's. She always said journaling was too much work, but she kept a diary in her own way. She had accounts on every kind of social media and busily photographed and posted the most mundane details of her daily life, especially if she encountered a stray animal or a particularly cute cup of coffee. Plus, her handwriting was a loopy, messy half cursive that was a headache to read. Whoever wrote this clearly took extra effort to make sure it was legible. It looked like it could have been typed, except for variations in the print size and the occasional inkblot.

The book was short, and it didn't take long to flip to the end. A perfect circle filled with odd shapes and symbols took up the entire last page. Most of it didn't make any sense to me, but a few looked like stick figures and stars. Below the circle, there was a drawing of a single lit candle, beside which were thick, block letters spelling: TRANSIET IN TENEBRAE.

Still examining that final page, I opened the bedroom door and went back to the couch.

"Where the hell did you get this?" I asked.

There was no answer. Emily was gone when I raised my head. I sighed. Searching her desk had gotten me so keyed up, I could've run a marathon. I was more awake than I'd been in almost a month, and she only appeared when I was beat. I'd have to wait until the high of excitement wore off.

The stink from the kitchen sink wafted over to me, pulled by the breeze from the open window.

"Might as well wear myself out," I muttered, turning on the faucet.

"This is a nice surprise." Zuri stood in the doorway and surveyed the apartment. "No dishes in the sink *and* I can actually see the floor?"

"I aim to please." I lay stretched out on the sofa, taking up all three cushions beneath my softest fleece blanket. I'd put the little brown book in my pillowcase for safekeeping. I could feel the ridge of it through the stuffing in my pillow.

She crossed the room to perch on the arm of the couch, took the mug out of my hand, and sniffed it. "Chamomile? Did you finally sell your stock in Super Energy Blast?"

"Just trying to relax." In truth, I was trying to bring myself back to the brink of falling asleep. The tea, the blanket, the home shopping channel that played on the TV—they were all part of a strategy that didn't seem to be working. Had I known this whole time that wanting to fall asleep was the secret to staying awake, I would've saved a fortune on energy drinks.

"I'm glad." Zuri's voice was soft, and she reached down to squeeze my foot. "I haven't wanted to say anything, but I've been worried about you."

I clenched my jaw and said nothing, despite the torrent of angry responses that flooded my mind. Zuri, like everyone else, was more worried about me than Emily. Like everyone else, she professed concern but didn't do much more than talk about it. But if I told her how I felt, we would get into an argument, and the adrenaline would keep me awake. So I lay there, staring at a spinning silver bracelet on the television screen, and kept quiet.

She sighed and set the mug down on the coffee table. "I know you think it's pity or something, but it's not. I miss you, Annie. You've been different since Emily got sick."

"She didn't get sick." I couldn't help it; the words leaped from my mouth. "She was taken."

"What are you talking about?"

"Nothing."

She slid off the armrest and rounded the couch to kneel in front of me. Her eyebrows were drawn together so tightly that, for a second, I thought she was angry. But when she spoke, her voice was as gentle as always.

"Okay, tough talk time," she said. "I've been trying to figure out how to have this conversation with you for weeks, but I couldn't find the right words. Well, screw the right words. Annie, you need help."

I narrowed my eyes at her. "Help?"

"You're not processing what happened to Emily in a healthy way. There are grief counselors—"

"Grief? She's not dead!"

"Well, she might as well be!" For the first time in the four years I'd known her, Zuri raised her voice to a near shriek. She grabbed one of my hands in both of her own, and her eyes filled with tears. "Don't you get it? She's probably never going to wake up. Every day she's in that coma, it's less likely she'll come back to us. We have to let go."

I yanked my hand out of her grasp. "Let go? How can you say that? She's our friend!"

"She *was* our friend. That's what I'm saying. Since the moment the paramedics wheeled her out of here, she's been gone. Can't you feel it?"

"Feel what?"

"She used to fill this whole place with light and energy." Zuri looked around the room with flat, sad eyes. "I can't feel her here anymore."

"Maybe you can't, but I can. I've seen her." Would she believe me if I told her Emily had been kneeling in exactly the spot Zuri now sat, just hours earlier? "I've talked to her."

"Oh, Annie." She sat back on her heels and let her hands fall into her lap. "Why didn't you tell me it'd gotten this bad?"

"When could I have told you? You're never home."

She pursed her lips. For a minute, I thought it was over, that I won the argument. It was a good thing too, because I was starting to shake, and I knew I'd already undone all the work I'd put into relaxing.

"I'm sorry," she said. "It's hard, being home. You weren't here when I found her. You get to remember her the way she was at breakfast, happy and bubbly. But every time I walk into this room, I see it all over again. The furniture was everywhere—even the rug was rumpled up by the TV—and she was just lying there." She pointed to the space in front of the fireplace. "It looked like she was sleeping, but when I checked for her pulse, there wasn't one. I thought she was dead. I can't remember calling 911, but I remember sitting there with her cold, still hand in mine."

I stared at her. She'd never talked about it before, not like this. To be honest, I hadn't been able to bring myself to ask. I didn't want to think about it. It was bad enough that Emily was unconscious in a hospital bed without dwelling on what put her there.

Zuri was right; I was lucky. I didn't envy that memory. Maybe Emily was lucky too—lucky I wasn't there and wasn't haunted by what I'd seen. I was able to be here, to see her.

I considered telling Zuri what I'd found and including her in the plan to bring Emily back, but her red-rimmed eyes and slumped shoulders made me suspect she needed sleep even more than I did. Guilt twisted in my stomach. I'd been so wrapped up in my own sadness that I hadn't been paying attention to hers.

"Can I get you anything?" I asked. "Want some of this tea?"

"There's only one thing I want," she said. "I want you to get help. I want you to be able to move on."

"Okay," I said. Compared to what I faced with Emily, Zuri's request was nothing. "I'm guessing you already have the name of somebody you want me to see, right? I'll call them tomorrow and make an appointment."

Zuri's eyes widened. "Really?"

"Really."

She jumped forward, pulled me into a tight hug, and whispered in my ear, "Thank you."

"Why don't you go lie down or something?"

She pulled away from me and shook her head. "I've got a planning meeting for the graduation concert. It's going to be really nice. They're going to dedicate a song to Emily." She ran the middle finger of each hand under her eyes, brushing away gray lines of running mascara. "I'm going to splash some water on my face and head back to campus."

While she cleaned up in the bathroom, I snuggled back down into the blanket and yawned. If she was that happy getting me to agree to see a counselor, I couldn't wait to see her face when Emily woke up.

AFTER ZURI LEFT and the sun began to set, I felt the familiar weight of sleepiness pressing down on me. I blinked, and when I opened my eyes, Emily stood in front of the fireplace. She was more translucent than before, and I could see every detail of the picture frames behind her.

"I found the book," I told her.

Her eyes lit up. "I knew you would."

I sat up and leaned forward with my elbows on my knees. "So how does this work? I read the words and you wake up?"

She shook her head. "I wish it were that easy. You need to stand in the circle, hold the candle, and speak the words. That will connect us, so you can pull me out of the darkness."

"The darkness?"

"I don't know how else to describe it. It's where he's keeping me. It's so dark here, so empty. I want to come home!"

I wanted to jump up and hug her, then remembered I couldn't. "It's okay, Em. I'm coming for you."

"Please hurry." Her form flickered, fading like a candle about to go out. "It's been nearly a month. I don't have much longer."

"What happens when—"

She disappeared before I could finish my question.

"Shit!"

I dived to the side and retrieved the book from my pillowcase. The circle and its odd symbols waited for me on the last page, but it was barely four inches tall. Emily said I should stand inside it. I needed to draw a much larger version, plus find a candle somewhere.

Swearing under my breath, I dashed into the kitchen and started rummaging through our junk drawer. There, among the rubber bands and spare charging cables, I found a candle shaped like the number two, left over from Emily's twenty-second birthday a few months before, along with a small box of matches.

"Aha!"

At the back of the drawer, my hand closed around a cold metal tube. It was a giant, black magic marker, the kind Zuri used to make posters for Student Council events. I had everything I needed, except somewhere to draw the circle.

I crossed back into the living room, twisting the marker between my fingers and racking my brain for something I could draw on. Regular paper was too small. Zuri might have some poster board in her room, or I could check the dumpster for an old cardboard box. Or to hell with it, I could draw on the floor. We'd lose our deposit when we moved out after graduation… Maybe I could cover it with the rug.

It wasn't even a rug, really. It was a thin piece of carpet the previous tenants left behind. I lifted the edge and saw a curved line, delicately carved into the scuffed hardwood beneath the rug.

It looked like a piece of a circle.

I dropped the corner back down with a slap, dragged the coffee table out of the way, and pulled the rug over the couch to fully expose the floor. I was right; it was a circle. The carving was faded, but some parts stood out clearly, especially in the lower-traffic areas like where the coffee table normally sat. There, I could easily make out a figure encased in a star that matched the last page in Emily's book.

Did she draw this? I bent down and ran my thumb along the edge of the design, feeling the smoothness of the floor that was barely marred by the shallow carving. It seemed old, like years of feet walking on top of it had sanded down the ridges and made the lines less severe. No, she hadn't carved it, but maybe she used it. I stood and walked forward, wondering how many of her steps I was retracing.

The instant my feet hit the center of the circle, the little hairs on the back of my neck twitched. I was close to something powerful. I suddenly wanted to leave the apartment, find Zuri at her meeting, and never return. I certainly didn't want to light the candle that threatened to slip out of my sweaty fingers, and the thought of speaking those foreign words made bile rise up in my throat. But when I closed my eyes, I saw Emily's fading figure and heard her plea for help.

She was depending on me. She'd stood by me for four years— four years of roller-coaster emotions, insane workloads, and living on a shoestring in the hopes that we'd have a better future. Now all she needed from me was one thing—one small thing, really: to swallow my fear and stick to the plan so she could have that future.

I gulped down the stomach acid, struck a match, and lit the candle. Holding it above my head, I spoke the words from the book, "Transiet in tenebrae." When my mouth closed over the final syllable, the candle blew out and the lights went dark above me. The room was lit only by the full moon shining through the open window. As I blinked, it began to fade until I stood in a blackness so complete that I couldn't make out my own hand in front of my face.

"Emily?" I whispered. My voice was strangely muffled, as though I were talking through a pillow. "Are you here?"

No reply. I wanted to vomit, faint, and run away all at the same time. Just as I was deciding that option number two was the best choice out of those three, a glowing orb appeared in my peripheral vision. It was moving, growing larger... or coming closer. It was hard to tell which. Soon, the light of the orb filled my entire field of vision, and what I saw inside made my heart swell.

"Emily!"

She lay on the floor of the orb, curled up in the fetal position. Unlike when she'd appeared to me earlier that day, this version of her looked like the one that lay in the hospital bed—thin, wasted, her normally curly hair matted against her forehead.

"Emily!" I shouted again. "I'm here!"

She opened her eyes and lifted her head, squinting at me from inside the glowing ball. "Annie? Is that you?"

"Come on," I told her. "I'm taking you home."

I reached forward to grab her hand and yank her out of her prison. As my fingers neared the edge of the glowing light, Emily's eyes widened. "No!" she shrieked.

But it was too late to stop my momentum. I touched the orb, and it exploded, blinding me with a flash of lightning and deafening me with a roar of thunder. My legs buckled beneath me, and I let out a cry of pain, echoed by Emily's screaming.

The light faded... faded... faded... into nothing.

EMILY DIDN'T HAVE LONG. Soon, I knew, she would become like the dozens of other husks in the orb with us. They'd been people, once. Now they looked like set pieces from a horror film about a mummy's tomb.

I'd spent days pounding at the glowing haze that surrounded us. It looked like little more than smoke but was as solid as steel. I was too weak for that now, too weak to fight. Instead, I sat on the floor of the orb and stroked Emily's hair, listening to her ragged breathing. Through the haze, I could make out Zuri sitting on the couch in our living room. She hugged a pillow to her chest and cried, her tears spilling onto my fleece blanket. My heart ached for her, for all of us, but there was nothing I could do. The demon had already taken my form, following Zuri and haunting her at her most exhausted. Soon enough, she would find the book, and she'd already seen the carving. Twice.

Emily was too weak to answer my questions, and I wondered what form the demon had taken to lure her here. Knowing her, I guessed it could've been anything from a scared puppy to a perfect stranger who needed help. No wonder she'd been the first to go.

And soon, she really would be gone. I'd sit here, alone, until Zuri fell for the demon's tricks. At least then I'd have someone to stroke my hair while I withered away in the darkness.

THE BUMP

One day, not too long ago, a boy and his family passed through town on their way to the coast. While his parents shopped for supplies, the boy wandered Main Street until he came upon a schoolyard. In the open space in front of the peaked yellow building, he found a group of children clapping and stomping around a low mound of dirt.

"Bump, bump," the children sang. "Humpity-jump. Who's next, who's next, beneath the lump?"

The children hopped as one, counterclockwise around the mound, and began the refrain again. "Bump, bump—"

"Hello," interrupted the boy. "What are you doing?"

The children stopped their song and stared at the boy for a while before a small girl in pigtails stepped forward out of the circle. Her eyes were shadowed by the bright sun overhead, but her friendly smile drew the boy in.

"Playing a game," she said. "Want to try?"

The boy had been traveling alone with his parents for some time and missed playing with people his own age. He took a

111

step forward, intending to join the game, but lost his nerve when he saw the other children's eyes. All were shadowed, no matter the direction they looked. One child tilted her head back as though to search for shapes in the clouds above, and still her eyes were impossible to see.

The boy's stomach twisted. "I-I'd better get back to my parents."

"But you're traveling." The girl in pigtails frowned. "You must play a round. For luck."

She grabbed his sleeve and tugged him toward the other children. The boy tried to pull away, but the little girl was stronger than she looked, and he soon found himself within the circle.

The boy didn't want them to think he was a scaredy-cat, so he asked, "How do you play?"

"We'll show you," she said, moving around the group to take the place directly across the circle from him.

"And how do you win?"

"You'll see," she teased.

At once, the other children began to clap, building a steady rhythm. Some stomped their feet into the ground, sending up puffs of dust in time with their clapping. Soon, the song began.

"Bump, bump. Humpity-jump. Who's next, who's next, beneath the lump?"

The boy caught on quickly, singing along and clapping his hands. At the end of each refrain, the group hopped to the right, rotating around the mound. The boy didn't understand how the game was won or lost, but he let the rhythm swallow him up and enjoyed the thrill of acceptance.

"Bump, bump. Humpity-jump," they sang.

A heavy cloud passed in front of the sun, darkening the schoolyard. The girl in pigtails grinned at the boy from across the mound, and he saw that her eyes hadn't been difficult to see because of shadows from the midday sun.

They were missing entirely.

He felt her hollow eyes looking at him, piercing deep into his soul. He stopped clapping and stared at the other children. None had eyes, yet all stared back.

"Who's next, who's next, beneath the lump?" they sang.

The children hopped together, but the boy was distracted. The child on his left collided with him, and he lost his balance, toppling forward onto the mound. His head hit a rock on the dirt, and he lay there in a daze for a minute before scrambling to his feet and running from the schoolyard. Behind him, the eyeless children laughed.

He found his parents in the same shop where he'd left them. He began crying the moment his mother caught sight of him.

"What's the matter?" she asked, kneeling to wipe the tears from her son's cheeks.

"I was playing in the schoolyard with some other kids." When he tried to remember what they'd looked like, his head pounded. There'd been something about their eyes.... "I fell."

"Are you hurt?"

He rubbed the top of his head. A lump was already growing there, and it was tender to the touch. "A little."

She tsked and smiled at him. "You'll be alright. Help me carry these bags."

That night in their hotel, the boy clutched at his head. The lump grew larger beneath his fingers, and when he closed his eyes, he saw the children in the schoolyard, staring at him through their empty sockets. He screamed and screamed, and his parents called for the doctor. The doctor examined the bump on the boy's head but didn't appear concerned.

"Ice and rest, that's all he needs," he told the boy's parents. "How did it happen?"

The boy's mother shook her head. "He was playing by the school and fell down."

"By the school?" The doctor frowned. "Well, no wonder he got hurt. That whole area's been a mess since the fire last year. We lost the school and several homes." He shook his head. "Too many lives... so many children. Most people steer clear, for good reason."

After a final reassurance that the boy would be fine after a good night's sleep, the doctor left.

As his parents slept, the boy tossed and turned. The goose egg on his head continued to grow, and he tried to call out to his parents. He opened his mouth, but only a whisper of the song came out. "Bump, bump. Humpity-jump. Who's next, who's next, beneath the lump?"

In the morning, his bed was empty. He wasn't in the hotel room or taking a bath or even playing in the stream behind the building. His parents couldn't find him anywhere, and soon a search party gathered to locate the missing boy.

As they looked, his parents walked down Main Street, passing the blackened and charred remains of the old schoolhouse. The yard was deserted, but a second bump now sat beside the first.

The building is long gone, but the bumps are still there

today. If you're brave enough to stand beside them, you can hear the children singing:

"Bump, bump. Humpity-jump. Who's next, who's next, beneath the lump?"

THE THING INSIDE
JACKY JENSEN'S GARAGE

Missy's bolt cutters pinched at the padlock on the garage's side door. When she pulled them away, a thin groove betrayed our unsuccessful efforts to cut the lock free. There was no walking away now. Even if we couldn't get in, Jacky Jensen would know somebody had tried to access his garage.

If he figured out who it was, we were dead. He'd dislocated my shoulder in this same driveway fifteen years ago, and that'd just been for "trespassing" on his property while trying to retrieve Missy's favorite Frisbee.

I rubbed my shoulder and cast a nervous glance at the dark street behind us. "Hurry up. They'll notice we're gone any minute."

Missy grunted and squeezed the bolt cutters again, bracing one handle against her chest and using both arms to pull the other toward her body. Her blonde curls fell into her face as she strained the muscles that earned her a scholarship to Southern Utah University. "It might... help...," she panted, "if you... push... too."

I silently disagreed. My palms were way too sweaty to grip anything. Besides, this had been her idea.

Well, not the part about the breaking into Jacky's garage. That was mine. But I'd wanted to go to Home Depot, get some industrial-strength bolt cutters, and then just take them back for a refund after. Missy vetoed me, insisting we use her dad's rusty old pair so there wouldn't be any retail security footage tying us to the crime.

Crime. The word sent a jolt of fear into my belly. What if Jacky bailed on the party and came home early? What if he called the cops?

"Screw this," I said. "Let's get out of here."

Missy shook her head and spoke through gritted teeth, still winded from the exertion of squeezing the bolt cutters. "Not without… a picture… of that thing."

The wind picked up as she worked, sending frigid December air down the back of my hooded jacket. I tugged my beanie down over my ears and wondered if the low temperature was making the metal stronger. Before I could chip my way through the layer of Smirnoff Ice that covered the memories of my freshman physics class, a snap and a clink signaled Missy's success.

She groaned and rubbed her sternum through her puffy winter coat. "Ugh, that hurt."

I stared at the break in the padlock's U-bolt, unsure if it would still be breaking and entering if we didn't actually *enter* the garage. Missy had no such reservations, quickly yanking the lock away and turning the handle.

"Wait." I pressed a hand against the door. "What if there's nothing in there?"

"Don't puss out on me, Leah."

"I'm not scared! I'm just being pragmatic. Jacky's a liar, and we both know it. Remember when he told us his drum kit cost a hundred grand? And then gave Bruce Higgins a concussion when he called bullshit?"

"This is different." Missy's cheeks burned, either from the cold or the alcohol or both. "If it wasn't true, Jacky would've been bragging about it to everybody. But I only overheard him whispering about it to Michael Birmingham in the bathroom because they didn't know I was behind the shower curtain."

I raised an eyebrow. "Don't tell me you still take shots in the bathtub at parties."

"Don't judge me! You know I don't like the face whiskey makes me make. The point is, Michael's dad works for Weber County Animal Control, so he has access to those trucks with all the cages, right? Jacky probably wants Michael to borrow one so they can move the monster." She scrunched up her face, frowning deeply. "Although… it is aquatic. I wonder if they'll stick a kiddie pool in the back of the truck or something to keep it wet."

I rolled my eyes. "It's not the Bear Lake Monster. That thing's an urban legend, and a lazy one at that. Like the thing in Loch Ness would have a cousin in Utah."

"Dude, it is so real! And I'm going to get a picture and sell it to TMZ." She pulled her phone out of her pocket and waved it in front of my face.

"Okay, you're officially too drunk for this. TMZ only cares about Hollywood. And besides, on the way over here you said this is the monkey-lizard those people saw up at the Huntsville cemetery."

"Well, Jacky did say something about hair all over the trunk of his car, so it could be the Huntsville Horror. But he's always been obsessed with the Bear Lake Monster, so it could be that." She shrugged. "One or the other, but probably not both."

I shook my head in mock sadness. "I cannot believe you seriously think there's either a prehistoric lake monster or some kind of mutant on the other side of this door. They're made up, Missy. Just stupid stories to scare stupid kids."

"Don't call me stupid." Her eyes flashed angrily. "And if you're so sure nothing's in there, why did you even come?"

I squeezed my shoulder, letting the tiny spike of pain from the old injury dispel the last traces of my earlier buzz. I suddenly remembered exactly why I'd been so eager to trade the warmth of Daniel Bayard's college-break Christmas party for committing a felony in the freezing cold. "Because Jacky Jensen is a sadistic monster, so on the off chance he really has something—or more likely some*one*—locked in that garage, I came to set them free."

Before the fear of being arrested could take hold, I yanked the bolt cutters out of her hand, sucked in a deep breath of icy air, and pulled open the door.

The dueling scents of lawn clippings and engine oil tickled my nose as I tiptoed into the darkness. Missy's footsteps sounded after me, followed by the soft swish of the door closing behind her. A heartbeat later, her cell phone flashlight swept across the cavernous space.

Like most people in our suburban Ogden neighborhood, Jacky's family clearly thought having a garage was less about protecting their cars and more about storing all the crap that couldn't fit into their house. Missy's light passed over two chest freezers, an enormous tool bench, a towering stack of plastic totes, and a bank-vault-style gun safe before settling on a large cube-shaped object covered with a blue tarpaulin.

Missy elbowed me and whispered, "What is that?"

"I don't know," I whispered back. "Could be anything."

"Go look under the tarp."

"*You* go look under the tarp."

Missy's retort died on her lips as a dry, rasping moan drifted across the garage from the cube in the corner. Something metal rattled, and the tarp shifted slightly.

Every hair on the back of my neck pressed upward against my beanie as a shiver that had nothing to do with the temperature shook my body. My hand closed around the door handle behind us.

"Help me…" a high voice croaked. "Please."

"Oh my God," I muttered, releasing the handle and sprinting across the concrete floor. I'd known Jacky was a monster, but this was beyond anything I had ever imagined him capable of doing.

Kidnapping a kid and stashing him under a tarp in his garage? That was pure evil.

Missy's light followed me, but she stayed within arm's reach of the door, half crouched like she was ready to leap outside at the next sign of danger. That same metallic rattle sounded again as my fingers closed around the edge of the tarp, and the sharp odor of bleach stung my eyes.

With a single yank, I pulled the tarp to the floor, revealing an enormous dog run with plywood lashed to the top, forming a makeshift cage. The flap of the falling fabric wafted the foul stench of urine and feces directly into my face. No amount of bleach could cover that smell, not when the source was exposed to open air. There was another underlying odor there too, something familiar. I gagged, remembering the way my fourth-grade classroom had smelled when we got lazy about cleaning the class turtle's cage.

As I tugged my scarf up over my nose, Jacky's prisoner darted out of the light with a shriek and huddled against the far corner. If he hadn't just begged for help, I would have assumed he was a large dog from the way he crouched on the ground.

"It's okay," I told him. "We're not here to hurt you." Then, without taking my eyes off his unhealthy shape, I called to Missy, "There's another lock here. Keep the light steady."

Either she didn't hear me or she wasn't capable of doing as I asked, because the light shook and shuddered, creating a muted strobing effect. The flashing made it a struggle to fit the blades of the bolt cutter over the small combination lock holding the cage's door closed.

The boy in the corner watched me as I worked. He hid his face behind oversize hands, trembling even harder than Missy. But he seemed to believe what I'd said, inching closer to me as I squeezed the bolt cutters. His outline was strangely fuzzy in the dim light, as though he was covered in a thick layer of cotton.

Or fur.

Bang! Bang! Bang!

The closed metal vehicle door at the front of the garage rattled.

"Hey, you little brats!" a deep voice roared from outside as someone pounded on the door a few more times. "I told you to stay off my property!"

Sweat erupted on my palms. I lost my grip on the bolt cutters, and they tumbled out of my hands, clattering to the ground at my feet. I whipped around as the overhead light switched on and the garage door's motor rumbled to life.

The door lifted open, revealing my childhood tormenter an inch at a time—pointed cowboy boots, too-slim jeans, a brown Carhartt jacket, and a face too twisted by cruelty to be handsome. Jacky Jensen stood with his hands on his hips, baring his teeth in a snarl.

"Well, well, well. I wondered where you two—" His voice cut off when his eyes landed on the uncovered cage behind me. Rage contorted his features, and a scream ripped from his throat as he lurched toward me. "You stupid bitch! Get away from it!"

I shrieked and ducked, instinctively covering my head with my arms as though this were some kind of impromptu earthquake drill.

Before Jacky finished crossing the garage, something snapped behind me. Metal clinked against metal.

Jacky's sprint slowed. I heard his footsteps falter and dared to look up at him as he skidded to a halt a few feet away from me. The blood drained from his face. His mouth fell open, and a low, frightened moan escaped his lips.

His horrified expression entranced me. I'd never expected to see him look the way he'd made me feel for my entire childhood. Hell, my entire *life*. He'd terrified me until the day I left for college, and only my years out of state had given me enough courage to step foot on his property again.

The cage's door creaked behind me, and the edge of it was suddenly visible at the corner of my vision. Then the beautiful image of Jacky's shocked face was obscured by the lean, dark shape that leaped over me and tackled Jacky to the floor.

Jacky's screams cut through the still night air. I watched, hypnotized, as the fur-covered boy clawed at his captor's face and hands. Blood spattered on the concrete floor. The stink of excrement intensified for an instant, and then I forgot to breathe.

All I could do was watch.

Missy's arms were around me then, hauling me to my feet and yanking me away from the cage. She shouted something I couldn't hear—couldn't process—and I let her pull me back to the side door we'd come through.

As my feet crossed the threshold, Jacky's wails of pain died down to a wet gurgle, then stopped completely.

I paused for one last look at the carnage in his garage. Now that he'd stopped moving, it was easier to make out the shape of the thing Jacky had locked in that cage. His proportions were all wrong; his arms were far too long and his legs far too short to be human. His entire torso was covered in thick black fur, but when he turned to face me, his features were strangely reptilian, sharp and knobby like a Gila monster.

The thing blinked at me, eyelids closing the wrong way over his slitted pupils. Then, with a final glance back in my direction, the Huntsville Horror shambled off into the night with Jacky Jensen's limp body in tow.

INGUMA WE TRUST

Z azpi felt the impact of his brothers' bodies as they collided with one another, knees cracking into skulls and fingers jabbing into eyes and mouths. He saw nothing, but he could imagine the chaos. Shrieks of surprise and pain filled the blackness of their oaken prison, and the seven of them were roughly thrown side to side a few more times before the motion stopped.

"Why do they always shake the box?" Hiru moaned beside him.

A low grumble of agreement spread through the darkness. No one had an answer. So little of what the large ones did made sense to any of them. Despite knowing that none of his siblings could see him, Zazpi shrugged his shoulders. Then, as he had done so many times in his long life, he pressed his fingertips up and down his limbs to check for any sign of serious injury. He found only minor scrapes, the kind that would heal within hours provided he could stay in the safety of the box.

Of course, a good shake was often followed by an opening and an order, as though someone thought Zazpi and his brothers needed to be awakened before they would comply. It was wholly unnecessary; the little imps never slept.

"Finish your story," Lau urged. "What happened to the dragon?"

Zazpi opened his mouth, ready to dive back into the epic tale he had been recounting, the one about a seven-headed dragon who terrorized a group of shepherds. It was an old story, one he had picked up centuries before and retold hundreds of times since. Lau and the others already knew the ending, but what else was there to do in the dark?

"Quiet," Bat ordered. "Do you think we were shaken for nothing? Zazpi, you have the best ears among us. Listen."

Together, they felt their way through the blackness to the front of the box, at the seam where the lid met the base. The wood was thinnest there, and if everyone kept their grumblings to themselves, sound trickled in from the outside world.

"*Kontuz!*" came a rough voice.

The Euskara word sent a thrill down Zazpi's spine. It had been many years since he had heard a large one speak his language.

"I know that word." Hiru clutched Zazpi's arm. "Do you recognize his voice?"

"No," Zazpi whispered, pressing his ear against the wood. "Now be quiet."

"Do not shake it," the voice continued.

"Sorry," said another. To Zazpi's ears, the second voice sounded younger than the first but still like that of a man. "I didn't realize. Did I hurt them?"

Something thumped on the box's lid.

"No!" The deep voice was sharp. "Do not open it. Not until you are ready to command them."

"I won't be commanding anyone," said the other. "I'm sending them to my ex-wife so she can tell them what to do."

"A very cruel trick to play."

"Cruel? I'm doing this to help her. To help my son."

A snort pierced the box. "That is what you think you are

doing, but improperly handled, these creatures ruin lives."

Zazpi frowned. Were the two men talking about him? It didn't seem possible. He, like all his kind, loved nothing better than a job well done. Working, keeping busy, fixing and cleaning things—these were the antidotes to boredom and the keys to a satisfying existence.

Silence fell outside the box, lasting long enough to encourage the imps to badger Zazpi with questions.

"They speak oddly. What are they saying?" Hiru whispered.

"Can you understand them?" Bost squeaked before Zazpi could reply.

"Of course I can," Zazpi snapped. "It's the same language our last *jauna* spoke. You all heard it. You all learned it."

"Yes," said Bat. "But you have always had the greatest gift for language."

"If I don't send them to her, my son won't have a life to ruin," the younger voice said. "Please. I've been looking for some way to protect him for months."

"Protect him from what?"

"I'm not sure, but I have an idea. Now, how much? And do you ship to the United States?"

Hiru tugged on Zazpi's arm. "What are they saying?"

"I don't understand all of it." Zazpi paused to process his thoughts. "But I think we have a new jauna."

Even saying the word lit a fire of excitement in his chest. Soon, they would be free from the darkness.

Soon, they would have a task.

Thomas's screams jerked Amaya into wakefulness, yanking her out of a nonsensical dream and thrusting her back into a living nightmare. She was out of the recliner and on her feet in an instant. A breath later, her pounding feet carried her up the stairs to her son's bedroom, where she was met by a closed door.

It had been open when she went downstairs for a glass of water. She was sure of it. She made a point to leave it that way, afraid that if she closed it, Thomas would wake up and find himself alone in his room, abandoned, afraid, and unable to do anything about it but scream. So she had left it open and gone to the kitchen, then sat down for a moment in the armchair— just for a moment, just for a taste of the peace she'd had before Glenn left. She kicked herself for falling asleep. There would be no peace now, not until well after dawn.

She threw open the door and found Thomas thrashing in bed. It was a familiar scene, one she'd seen every night for the past six months. He had always been prone to nightmares. Glenn indulged him, checking beneath the bed and in the closet for monsters. For a while, it worked.

But not anymore.

Nothing she did kept the nightmares away now. Thomas woke up screaming every night, sitting up and kicking his Spider-Man blanket onto the ground before shouting, eyes closed, for his father.

"Help! Daddy, help!" Thomas yelled.

Amaya sat on the edge of his bed and wrapped an arm around him. "Shh, it's okay. You're okay. Mommy's here. Everything's fine."

Thomas's eyes were unfocused as he stared around the room. When his gaze landed on Amaya's face, he collapsed against her. "Mommy," he croaked. "Where were you?"

"I'm sorry, sweetie. I was just getting some water. But I'm here now. I'm right here."

He nodded and clutched at her nightshirt. Then, with a hiss, he lifted the corner of his Transformers pajama top. "Something hurts."

Amaya wasn't surprised. Thomas tended to bruise his arms

against the bedside table as he flailed in his sleep. She guessed he had pulled a muscle while contorting himself to get away from whatever monster his imagination cooked up in his dreams.

"Here, let me see." She leaned over and examined his skin.

A strangled gasp caught in her throat. Angry purple marks dotted the bottom of Thomas's rib cage, each cluster of four arching like—

Claw marks, she realized.

It looked as though someone had reached out to Thomas as he slept and dug their nails into her son's flesh. Only the marks were too round for that; fingernails would have left little half-moon divots. These circular bruises brought to mind images of spiked medieval torture devices.

Without another thought, Amaya gathered Thomas into her arms and bolted down the stairs, not stopping until they reached the kitchen. There, she rested him on the counter and snatched the phone from the wall. Even at the discounted rates, this call would cost a fortune, but she didn't care.

The long-distance line crackled and fuzzed.

"Come on, pick up," she murmured.

Glenn didn't answer. Amaya slammed the receiver down onto the hook with a discordant clang and glanced at Thomas. Terror strained the boy's features, and his eyes were more sunken and dull than any five-year-old's should ever be. She thought about the marks on his chest. Were they worth a trip to the emergency room?

No, she decided. He was breathing fine, his coloring was healthy, and he didn't have a fever. Whatever this was, it could wait until morning, when she could try to get him into his regular pediatrician.

"Come on," she said. "Let's watch a movie."

Within a few minutes, she had situated Thomas on the couch with a blanket and a mug of warm milk and slid his favorite

Disney cassette into the VCR. Her mind was too keyed up to focus on the cartoon, so she plucked a paperback Glenn had left behind off the shelf and started reading. Thomas snuggled up beside her, head resting on her chest where she could stroke his thick curls with her free hand.

Amaya was fifteen pages in and regretting her choice—why didn't Glenn ever warn her away from reading Stephen King after dark?—when a soft knock came at the door. She detached herself from Thomas and answered it, finding her neighbor on the porch with a package in her hands.

"Hey, Amaya, sorry it's so late." Jennifer, who lived across the street, grimaced apologetically. "I saw the light from your TV and figured you must still be awake."

"It's no problem. Thomas had a nightmare, so we're up. What's going on?"

"This got delivered to my house by mistake." Jennifer handed Amaya the package.

It was about the size of a shoebox and covered in stickers and stamps from the delivery service. Amaya's curious gaze locked on to the Spanish postmark, and her body stiffened.

Glenn was in Spain.

"It looked important, so I wanted to get it to you right away." Jennifer paused and studied Amaya's face. "Hey, are you okay?"

"Fine," Amaya murmured, still staring at the postmark.

Without another word, she stepped backward and closed the door on Jennifer. She hadn't heard from Glenn in months—not a single reply to any of her letters, nothing at all since he called to let her know that he and his new family had relocated to Madrid. Or were they his old family, since the children he'd kept secret from her were older than Thomas?

She ground her teeth. Moving to Spain had been her dream. While pregnant with Thomas, she looked into what it would take to emigrate, hoping her ancestry would be enough to shortcut the process. Glenn had laughed and told her if she wanted a fast track to citizenship, she should have married a Spaniard.

Five years later, he took his own advice.

"Who was that, Mommy?"

Amaya spun around. Thomas stood behind her, his blanket trailing behind him and a milk mustache on his lip.

"It was Jennifer." Amaya lifted the box and forced a smile. "We got a package."

Thomas's eyes lit up with interest. The lure of an unopened box was too much excitement for even his nightmares to dampen.

"Can I help you open it?" he asked.

"Sure, sweetie."

With Thomas bouncing on the chair beside her at the kitchen table and her car key in hand, she paused before slicing the packing tape open. The sender's address wasn't in Madrid; it listed a street in Bilbao, up on the northern coast where her great-aunts and uncles lived. Could the package be from one of them—a belated birthday present for Thomas or some old photos from one of Amaya's childhood visits to the family farmhouse?

The possibility of finding a gift from someone who still loved her gave her the courage to rip her key down the tape. Thomas stood up on his chair, pulled the flaps open, and retrieved a folded piece of paper from inside. He opened it and thrust it at her with a distasteful frown.

"It's in cursive," he complained.

As soon as Amaya saw the handwriting, she knew this wasn't from any of her distant family. The letter was in Glenn's jagged, narrow penmanship. She slumped back against her chair with a sigh and scanned it.

Amaya—

Thank you for keeping me informed about Thomas. I talked to Victoria about it, and she (in jest, though well-meaning) suggested it might be more than nightmares that plague him. That sent me down a path I haven't trod since my graduate research in Southern France, and I found something I think may help. As a Vasco, you should be able to use it.

There are three things you must remember. First, don't open the box until you have a command ready. Second, don't let them get bored. And last, to get them back into the box, fill it with ash and tell them to clean it.

Write me if things get worse. Tell Thomas I love him.
Regards,
Glenn

Amaya's nails pierced through the back of the page as she squeezed the letter. There was so much wrong with it, she didn't know where to start. Like everything else to do with Glenn, it was all flowery pomp and no substance. What had he sent her? Why did he think it would help? Was she only supposed to write him if things got even worse? What if they got better?

Packing peanuts bounced off the tablecloth as Thomas lifted something else out of the cardboard. He set it onto the table with care and looked up at his mother. "What is it?"

Amaya crumpled the letter and let it fall to the floor, then leaned forward to help her son. She brushed a few stubborn bits of Styrofoam from the top of the box and frowned at it. It looked like something she might find at an antique store, and the aroma of polished wood awakened memories of childhood visits to her family. Someone had carved a single word into the top in bulging, bulbous script: *Galtzagorriak*. She knew the word and decided Glenn must have sent some toys to Thomas, as though that would erase any of the psychological damage he caused by abandoning his son.

"Go ahead, sweetie," she said. "Open it up, and we'll see."

ZAZPI HELD HIS BREATH. He recognized the side-to-side rocking of being carried and the heavy thump that signaled their box had been set down onto a flat surface. He and his brothers readied themselves, miniature muscles tensing as they crouched.

Yellow light flooded the box, blinding their eyes as the hinged lid lifted and the magical seals trapping them broke. Bat, the eldest, threw a small pouch down onto the wood at their feet. It burst open with a loud pop as the other six imps braced their backs against the lid, pressing against it with all their might. Black smoke filled the surrounding space, momentarily blocking out the light as the Galtzagorriak exploded out of their prison.

As the smoke cleared, the imps oriented themselves in their surroundings. They stood on a square wooden surface many times larger than their box. From the smell of toasted bread and the sink against the wall, Zazpi guessed they were in a kitchen. That wasn't unusual; for whatever reason, they were nearly always released in kitchens—that, or on low tables surrounded by couches. Bat had a theory that the large ones liked to meet the imps where they were most comfortable, in an area of their homes that they used frequently, but Lau maintained it depended on where in the home the wine was kept.

Zazpi glanced behind himself to be sure his brothers were ready and had arranged themselves properly. They stood in a line, three to either side, cheeks flushed with excitement, eyes looking upward at the enormous faces that squinted down at them through the rapidly fading smoke.

Both were faces much like their own, round and framed by dark curls. The woman was pretty, Zazpi decided. A boy sat beside her, several missing teeth visible in his gaping mouth.

"*Kaixo!*" Zazpi greeted them.

The large ones stared at him blankly, neither one responding.

Zazpi threw a panicked glance at Bat, who shrugged and urged the young imp forward with the backs of his hands. He tried again, switching to the language he had last heard outside their box. "Hello?"

The woman's pupils contracted, and she blinked a few times. The boy beside her grinned.

"Look, Mommy! Red pants, like in the story!" The child held out a cautious finger as though he expected Zazpi to bite him. "My name's Thomas. What's your name?"

"Zazpi," the imp said, relieved at least one of them was speaking. "We are at your service. What are your orders, jauna?"

Thomas pealed with laughter. "He's funny. Can we keep him?"

The woman shook her head violently and slapped her cheeks with both hands. When she looked at Zazpi again, her eyes remained as wide and shocked as they had been since the smoke cleared.

"I don't believe it," she said. "This can't be real. You're just a story."

Zazpi brightened. "A story? I will tell you one. Long ago, deep in the mountains—"

The sound of shattering glass made Zazpi jump. He peered around the woman to find what had caused it. Hiru had left the table and climbed on top of a tall shelf. Pieces of a broken wine glass covered the floor, and Hiru was inching another toward the edge.

"A mess!" Bi exclaimed. "I will clean it!"

"And I will fix the glass!" Bat shouted as he dived off the side of the table. He was a blur of red and white as he flew across the floor at top speed to get to work.

Thomas tugged on his mother's sleeve. "They're bored, Mommy. Remember the story?"

Zazpi was indeed growing bored. Fluffy white chunks of an

unfamiliar material covered the table, and he had a sudden urge to tear them into tiny pieces and try to put them together again. The glow from the yellow light bulb above him offered another potential task; he could climb up there and smash it, then clean up the little shards of glass he imagined would rain down on the kitchen.

"Stop!" the woman shouted.

Her order echoed, English in Zazpi's ears and Euskara in his mind. He turned and relayed the word to his brothers, who froze where they stood.

"I need you to…." The woman narrowed her eyes and frowned around the room. "Deep clean the entire house. Top to bottom. I don't want to see a single speck of dirt or dust anywhere inside."

"*Bai*, jauna!" Zazpi turned to leap off the edge of the table.

"Wait." She held out an enormous hand, blocking his path, and repeated his last word. "How-nah? What is that?"

Zazpi concentrated and tried to recall the word his previous jauna had told them to use. "Boss."

She shook her head. "I'm nobody's boss. Just call me Amaya, okay?"

"Amaya. I will do so. Shall I start?"

"Hold on." She leaned toward him, so close he could smell the lingering traces of watermelon from her shampoo. "Is it true you'll do whatever I ask?"

"Anything that is within our power, and we have many skills. What do you need?"

Her eyes bored into Zazpi's, dark and serious. "Protect my son."

IT HAD TAKEN until the wine glass shattered for Amaya to dredge up the details of the old stories from the back of her mind. They used to be some of Thomas's favorites, but like so many other things, the boy lost interest after Glenn left. He'd pulled down the drawings he'd made of the Galtzagorriak from his bedroom walls, throwing the stick figures with red legs and long pointed ears into the garbage.

The creature standing on Amaya's table now looked just as she always imagined. He could have fit in her palm, and he wore red pants and a white tunic made from some rough, homespun material. She wasn't sure if his ears were as long as Thomas had drawn them, as they were hidden by a wide black beret. He looked harmless, but the warning from Glenn's letter was the same in those old stories: *Don't let them get bored.*

She tried to follow the thread of Glenn's logic. Clearly, he had remembered the stories. But instead of dismissing them as fairy tales the way an ordinary person would, the king of the double life had hunted these creatures down. She assumed he was proud of his work, patting himself on the back before putting the issue out of his mind.

Glenn had never been a fan of the simple solution, except for the time he fixed the problem of having two families by completely abandoning one of them. But that didn't automatically mean he wasn't on to something here.

And what did she have to lose?

She told the little man what she really wanted. The only thing she needed. "Protect my son."

"From what?" he asked in a piping voice. Zazpi, that was the name he'd given Thomas.

Amaya glanced down at the boy, who stared at Zazpi with enraptured eyes, his nightmares forgotten for the moment. But Amaya hadn't forgotten—and could never forget—the angry purple bruises that lurked beneath his pajama top.

What had made them? He couldn't have done it himself. His fingers were too small. If Glenn were still here, she would wonder if he'd made them. And she suspected that if she took Thomas to the doctor in the morning, the pediatrician would assume she had done it.

But as she stared at the tiny man, who by rights shouldn't even exist, she began to understand Glenn's logic. What if it wasn't just nightmares that sent her son shooting upright in bed every night, screaming in terror? What if there was something she couldn't see—something unnatural?

Unnatural problems deserved unnatural solutions.

Zazpi was looking at her expectantly, but she didn't have an answer to his question.

"I need you to watch him," she said. "Keep an eye on him while he sleeps. Maybe you won't see anything, but I want you to keep watch regardless."

"Bai, Amaya."

"You won't fall asleep?"

He shook his head. "We never sleep."

She studied him, searching for any flaws in her plan. "And you won't get bored?"

Zazpi hesitated. "I will only be watching—not working?"

"Well, watching can be working," Amaya said. "There are lots of jobs like that, like security guards. They just look out for trouble and keep things safe."

"But only watching?" Zazpi repeated. "Not... doing?"

There it was, the technicality she'd been worried about. After a moment's hesitation, she went into the living room and returned with the book she'd been reading before Glenn's package arrived. It was heavy, several times larger than the box containing the Galtzagorriak.

"You like stories, right?" she asked. "Come on. This will keep you busy while you watch us."

Zazpi liked Thomas a great deal. The boy was far more excited to see him than any jauna Zazpi could remember and sat up in his bed, asking the imp to tell him stories about the things he had seen and done over the course of his long life. Amaya sat beside Thomas with one arm looped around his shoulders. At her command, Zazpi chose only tales with happy endings.

Before long, Thomas's questions grew further apart, and as the boy yawned, Amaya clicked off the lamp. She scooted down in the bed with her head propped up on a folded pillow, and Thomas rolled over on his side. Zazpi watched him with interest. He had never watched a large one sleep. These were the hours during which he and his brothers got the most work done, and he wondered now what it would feel like to close his eyes and let the world fade away into nothing around him.

"Is that enough light to read by?" Amaya whispered, nodding toward the dog-shaped light glowing above the dresser.

"Bai."

"Good. I'll try to stay awake too."

Zazpi nodded and got to work on the other task she had set him. The book was thick, and his progress was slow. There were many words he didn't understand and things he found impossible to picture. But he thought Hiru would be interested in the wax that made things waterproof and looked forward to telling his brothers about it the next time they were locked in their box.

As Zazpi slid off the book to turn the large page, Thomas stirred. A frightened squeak slipped out from between his lips, and Zazpi glanced up at him.

Something sat atop the boy's stomach.

A shadow perched there, its legs tucked beneath itself like a cat crouched over a mouse hole, and its body rose and fell in time with Thomas's belly as he breathed. Zazpi glanced to the side without moving his head to check on Amaya. Her head tipped forward at an uncomfortable angle, and a low snore drifted across the room.

Zazpi's gaze returned to the shadow. He didn't know if this was normal for large ones as they slept, for a creature like this to appear without warning and lurk over them in the darkness. Just because this was the first time Zazpi had seen it didn't mean it didn't happen every night.

As he watched, the thing bent forward, its face mere inches from Thomas's mouth. It whispered something Zazpi couldn't understand. Thomas moaned. The creature flexed, its body tensing as its back feet dug into Thomas's chest for purchase.

"Hello," Zazpi began, thinking he needed more information before deciding if he should wake Amaya. "What are you doing?"

The shadow jerked its head to the side. With a movement faster than even Zazpi could manage, the creature leaped to the end of the bed, reached out a colorless claw, and plucked Zazpi from his place on the dresser. The imp hung there, the back of his tunic pinched between two needles at the ends of a pair of long, knobby fingers.

"Galtzagorria," the shadow hissed. Sharp white teeth emerged from the shapeless depths of its face. "I didn't think there were any of you left. Tell me, what are you doing here?"

The question echoed in Zazpi's mind the way only an order from his jauna should, and he answered automatically. "I am protecting Thomas."

A low, raspy chuckle oozed from the creature's throat. "There is no stopping me. Surely you know that."

"I don't even know what you are," Zazpi admitted.

"Don't you recognize your own kin? Though you never sleep and have no dreams, you must know who I am."

Sleep. Dreams. A memory surfaced of a story Zazpi never told his brothers, one which didn't interest them. Only those who could dream had reason to fear the Lord of Nightmares.

Zazpi named him in his own tongue. "*Inguma zara.*"

"I am. And you"—Inguma lifted Zazpi higher into the air—"are an insect. But even insects can be useful. Leave me to my business, and I will reward you. You and your brothers can serve me in the night, the way your kind once served my brethren. You will never be bored."

"We already have a jauna." Zazpi glanced once more at Amaya, who still snored beside her son.

"But how much do you help your masters? The large ones, you call them. But you give them too much credit for their size. They are small creatures, both of heart and mind. Without the dreams I feed them, they would amount to nothing."

"Is that what you were doing to Thomas? Feeding him dreams?"

"Yes, among other things." The line of Inguma's jagged teeth curled upward. "I see the concern in your eyes. What a loyal servant you are. But do not mistake his cries of fear as cries for help. I'm already helping him. Humans need fear in their lives. What is happiness without grief? Joy without pain? Most of them would never raise a single foot to run without something chasing them. Come with me and help me motivate them to greatness."

Inguma's words echoed. *Come with me.* The command was there, so easy to follow, and it carried with it a temptation greater even than the urge to create work for himself. If Zazpi accepted, he would never be bored. He would have an eternal jauna and never again be forced to wait in his prison until he was needed.

As Zazpi considered the offer, Thomas twitched. The features of the boy's face were still twisted in fear. He shuddered and clawed at the air, battling some unseen terror. Was that the future Inguma offered? Forcing the large ones to suffer in the night?

And Thomas was suffering. Zazpi could see that now. Inguma might be able to command him, but Zazpi had only one true jauna. And her orders were clear.

"Brothers!" he shouted. "Help me protect Thomas!"

"Fool!" Inguma spat. "The boy is mine. I have marked him. If you can't break your chains, I'll break them for you."

With a snap of shadowed fingers, Inguma summoned Zazpi's box into the air beside him. Its lid hung open, just as it had while sitting on the kitchen table downstairs. Zazpi winced, sure the ancient god intended to force him into the box and lock him in the darkness forever.

Instead, Inguma gripped the oaken container in his free hand and squeezed. The wood groaned in protest, but it couldn't hold out against Inguma's strength. It crumbled into pieces between his fingers. As they fell to the bed, a wall of force nearly knocked Zazpi out of Inguma's grasp.

"I have need of your brothers," Inguma said. "They are bound to me now. But you.... You will pay for your defiance."

He brought Zazpi to his mouth, and the imp cringed away from the clear fluid dripping down the shards of Inguma's teeth. But rather than devour him, Inguma exhaled onto him, sending a thick cloud of lavender-scented mist swirling around Zazpi's small body.

Zazpi's eyelids grew heavy. Inguma whispered something the imp couldn't understand. Then, with a flick of his wrist, he hurled Zazpi across the room, back toward the dresser and the unfinished book.

Just before he hit the wall, Zazpi slipped into unconsciousness.

AMAYA WOKE to the sound of Thomas's screams. She shoved against the mattress beneath her, forcing herself into a rough sitting position as she fought to gain her bearings. Thomas was beside her, kicking at the comforter and thrashing his arms. She caught hold of him, and soothing sounds poured from her mouth until he blinked his eyes open.

"It's okay, honey," she crooned. "Mommy's here. You're

okay. It was just a dream."

Once again, she berated herself for dozing off. How could she? But as she lectured herself, she felt the heaviness of exhaustion pressing against her.

Of course she'd fallen asleep. Even now, she was desperate for more, just eight solid hours to reset to normal. Her only mistake was not telling Zazpi to wake her if—or rather, when—she nodded off.

Thomas whimpered and touched his chest. "It hurts."

"Let me see."

She lifted the front of his pajama shirt and inhaled sharply. Even in the dim light from the rising dawn, it was easy to see that the bruises across his rib cage were larger than before. The purple hue had deepened, and white scratches surrounded the marks as though something with claws had been scrabbling for purchase before they dug in.

Amaya's mind raced through the possibilities of what could have attacked Thomas without waking her. Her mind raced from mountain lions to unseen terrors. Things that only came out at night. Things she'd never believed in until that moment.

"That's it." She sprang to her feet and bent to scoop Thomas up. "We're getting out of here."

It was then she noticed the debris on the bed. Irregular chunks of wood were scattered across the comforter. She frowned down at one of the larger pieces, which had a bulbous letter *G* carved into it, then jerked her head up and scanned the dresser. She was sure that's where Zazpi had been sitting, but she saw no sign of the imp.

Thomas whimpered again, and Amaya lifted him into her arms. As she passed the dresser, a flash of red caught her eye. Zazpi lay there, his tiny body crumpled in a heap behind the Stephen King paperback. He didn't look injured, and his miniature chest rose and fell evenly.

"Zazpi," she said. "Wake up."

He didn't respond. She poked him with a finger, and he stirred slightly, only to curl into an even tighter ball with an agitated sigh.

"Is he hurt?" Thomas asked.

"I don't know."

Thomas tightened his arms around her neck. "Is he coming too?"

Amaya wasn't sure where they were going, but it couldn't hurt to have a magical helper along.

"Sure, baby." Amaya picked up Zazpi and handed him to Thomas, who cradled the imp with care. "Now, let's go find your suitcase."

AN AGONIZED WAIL ripped its way out of Zazpi's throat. Pain seared up and down his body.

"Stop!" he begged. "Please, please stop!"

His brothers didn't listen. Their eyes were hollow, devoid of the joy and laughter he was used to seeing in them. They dragged their nails down his skin like claws, pulling the flesh from his bones one strip at a time.

Bat shook his head. "We cannot stop. You brought this upon yourself."

Then, without knowing how, Zazpi was on his feet. His brothers were behind him, shouting and chasing after him. He stumbled forward. His legs felt sluggish and refused to move. What was wrong with him? Why couldn't he fly forward with his normal speed?

His feet tangled. He tripped, falling forward. The ground opened beneath him, cracking into a wide chasm. At first, it seemed to have no bottom. Then one appeared, just a blip at first. It grew at an impossible speed as it rushed toward his face. He screamed, flailing his arms, struggling to brace for impact when there was nothing to brace against—

He woke with a gasp. Sweat matted his curls to his forehead, and his arms were tangled in a blanket. He sat up slowly, blinking against the flickering sunlight through the window. Above him, Thomas's enormous face lit up with joy.

"He's awake, Mommy!" the boy said.

Awake. Goose bumps marched across Zazpi's body as the reality of what he had just experienced sank in.

He had slept.

He had dreamed.

"No," he whispered.

It wasn't possible. By his very nature, he never slept. If he could do it now, what did that make him? Was he still himself? Was he still Zazpi?

The memory of Inguma crushing the oaken box played through his mind. He had shared that home with his brothers for millennia, and now it lay in pieces across Thomas's bed. Was that why he had fallen asleep? Because the box had been destroyed? What did that mean? Where would they live when they weren't needed?

There were too many questions. He needed to know the answer to at least something.

"Where are we?" he asked Thomas.

"In the car. Wanna see?"

"No." Zazpi shuddered and shifted into a sitting position on Thomas's lap. He had been in an automobile before and hadn't liked the speed at which the surrounding scenery passed. "Are my brothers here too?"

"I couldn't find them," Amaya said from the front seat. "They wrecked the house and left."

"We saw holes in the walls, and the kitchen floor is gone," Thomas said.

Amaya sighed. "Yeah. They ripped out all the linoleum. I thought for sure I gave them enough to do for a few hours."

Zazpi frowned. It was true; her order had been large enough to keep the six of them busy until well past dawn. And even if they ran out of work, there were ways to make more. Left to their own devices, he and the others spent days tearing things apart and weeks putting them right again. A box full of ash always waited for them at the end, but they would never leave their master's home unless ordered to do so.

Unless....

"They're really gone," he whispered.

Inguma hadn't been lying. He had bound Zazpi's brothers to him, leaving the youngest imp behind.

Alone.

He flung himself back against Thomas's stomach. The boy cried out in protest, and Zazpi sat forward again. "I'm sorry."

"Be careful of his bruises," Amaya said. "They're bigger now."

Thomas lifted his shirt, and Zazpi's eyes widened.

"Inguma's marks." He reached out a hand, then thought better of it and hugged his fist to his chest. "That's what he meant."

"What?" Amaya's head whipped to the side, and the motion of the car slowed. When it stopped, she turned around in her seat to face Zazpi. "Did you see something last night? Tell me what happened, Zazpi!"

He told her all he could recall, not just seeing Inguma crouched on Thomas's bed the night before, but all he knew from the stories he had heard the large ones tell.

"Inguma is an ancient god, older even than any of my brothers. He is the bringer of nightmares. I've heard large ones say—" Zazpi swallowed, remembering the way Inguma had hunched over Thomas's sleeping body. "They said that when someone died in their sleep, it was because Inguma claimed them."

The thought had once brought him comfort. He didn't sleep. He had been certain that so long as he never slept, he could never die.

Amaya looked stricken. Desperation filled her eyes, and she reached behind her seat to snatch Zazpi off Thomas's lap.

"How do we stop him?" She shook Zazpi, gripping him with both hands. "Tell me!"

"I don't know," he cried. Then a terrifying realization hit him.

His jauna had just given him a command. *Tell me.* It should have echoed in his mind, cementing his drive to complete the task he'd been given.

But it didn't. The truth broke over him like the sea over a ship.

He had no jauna.

He had no purpose.

He had no brothers.

His body sagged, going limp in Amaya's grasp, and he wept.

AMAYA DIDN'T KNOW MUCH, but she had a solid handle on one thing: if she ever saw Glenn again, she would kill him.

Her mind kept trying to drift into anxiety and worry, but as she put as much distance as she could between Thomas and the thing haunting his bedroom, the hatred gave her something else to focus on. She imagined flying to Spain, tracking Glenn down, and punching him right in his smug face. She couldn't believe she'd allowed herself to put any faith in the so-called solution he'd sent her. How disconnected from reality was he to send her magical imps? It shouldn't have surprised her. As per usual, his attempts to help only made her life worse. Now, on top of having to figure out how to protect her son from some forgotten deity, she had to deal with a demolished townhome.

Zazpi was no help. When he finally stopped crying, she asked him to help her keep Thomas awake with stories or car games, but the imp lay on the passenger seat, eyes wide, staring at the sedan's cloth ceiling. She understood his grief—it sounded like he might never see his family again—but she couldn't spare much thought for how to help him cope with his new reality. Her only priority was the safety of her son.

At least her plan seemed to be working so far. Thomas dozed off after a drive-through dinner, but either this Inguma creature couldn't get to him outside their house, or he couldn't keep up with a car on the freeway. There were no signs of nightmares on Thomas's face, and he slept quietly.

The bigger problem was her own fatigue. She couldn't keep driving forever. And if she fell asleep at the wheel and they plowed into the concrete barrier at sixty-five miles an hour, she would be doing Inguma's work for him.

Reluctantly, she pulled off the freeway a little after midnight and found a motel.

"Wake up, sweetie," she whispered to Thomas as she unbuckled his booster seat. "Isn't this fun? You've always wanted to stay somewhere with a pool."

He rubbed a fist across one eye and squinted sleepily at the motel's neon sign. "Is Zazpi staying here too? Can he swim with me?"

Amaya glanced at the imp, who was still on his back, limbs flung in all directions. "If he wants. But it's his choice."

"Come on, Zazpi," Thomas encouraged. "Come play with me."

Zazpi moved in slow motion, as though his body was bogged down by a thick layer of molasses, but he climbed off the seat and into Amaya's purse. Thomas wanted to be in charge of the roller bag, so she let him drag it behind them from the car to their room, hoping the excitement of being in a motel would help keep him awake. Along the way, she paused at a vending machine to buy a few cans of off-brand cola.

Soon, Thomas was settled onto one of the room's two beds with a can of soda and a coloring book. Amaya called the front desk and requested a wake-up call for three o'clock.

"Three a.m.?" the clerk asked uncertainly.

"Yes, three a.m.," she repeated. "Can you do that?"

He confirmed he would, and she hung up and slid beneath the covers on the second bed. She just needed a few hours of sleep, followed by a caffeine pick-me-up.

Then they would keep moving.

Zazpi wondered if he should get out of Amaya's purse. He thought about it for a good while but couldn't come up with a convincing argument. His brothers wouldn't be waiting for him. He had no jauna and no work to do. What was the point?

The answer was easy. There was no point.

He settled for rearranging himself so her keys weren't jabbing him in the back and went back to staring up at the ceiling. The textured plaster was framed by the light brown edges of Amaya's purse, and it almost looked like one side was the lip of his oaken box and the other side was the lid. He wished he could burst out of it in a puff of Bat's smoke, ready and eager to do whatever was asked of him.

Tears filled his eyes. He couldn't imagine ever feeling that way again.

The light above him flickered. A moment later, it went out.

"Amaya?" he called.

No answer came.

"Thomas?"

Still nothing.

Unease crept up his spine. He had heard Amaya tell Thomas she would leave the light on while she napped, that he would be safe until she woke up. Had Thomas turned the lights off by himself? Was that why he wasn't crying out in the dark?

Zazpi couldn't keep lying there without knowing the answer. Curiosity and dread motivated him to climb out and check Thomas's bed.

Inguma crouched there, his shadowed body bent over Thomas's sleeping form. "Hold the boy," he said. "He's a strong one. Don't let him kick me off before I can pierce his soul. I need to reach it before dawn."

Six small figures emerged from the shadows and crept toward the boy, each wearing a black beret.

Zazpi sucked in a breath. "Brothers! You're here!"

He clambered down out of the purse and zipped over to the bed, bounding onto the rough blanket. He expected his brothers to greet him warmly, for Hiru to wrap him in a hug and for Bat to lecture him for not coming with them the night before.

They ignored him. Silently, they flanked Thomas, three to each side.

"Ah, it's you." Inguma dug his claws into Thomas's chest and flashed his teeth at Zazpi. "Did you enjoy your dream? I made it just for you."

Zazpi stared at the white talons, remembering the bruises they had left on Thomas and the way the boy cried out in pain when Zazpi knocked against them. And, for the first time since he'd awoken from that terrible nightmare, he wanted to do something.

He wanted to help Thomas.

"Stop that," Zazpi said. "Stop hurting him."

"I told you, the boy is mine. I marked him. Leave or pay the price for staying."

"No." Zazpi drew himself up to his full four inches. "Stop or I'll make you stop."

Inguma chuckled. "You are powerless, imp. There is nothing you can do."

Zazpi barely heard the words. He was already running, flying around the room as fast as his legs would carry him. He wanted to laugh at his own stupidity—he had forgotten an important truth, one that had driven him to branch out from their jauna's orders time and again: if there was no work to do, he could make his own.

He darted along Thomas's bed, pulling the comforter behind him. It peeled back from the boy, knocking Inguma off-balance. He'd been hoping to send Inguma tumbling to the floor, but the old god regained his footing and sunk his claws back into the boy's chest.

"Wake up!" Zazpi shouted, running across Thomas's face and leaping onto Amaya's pillow. He clapped his hands onto her nostrils, sealing them between his palms. "Wake up!"

Amaya gasped and shot up, hair wild and eyes darting. "What? What is it?"

Zazpi stopped moving to answer and was tackled off the bed. Lau, Bost, and Sei grappled him to the floor. Zazpi scratched at Sei's face, expecting him to cry out in pain, but his brother made no sound. Sei's eyes were dull and lifeless, and his motions were as jagged as a puppet on a string.

"Sei," Zazpi whispered. "Are you in there?"

Sei didn't answer. He pinned Zazpi down while the other two wrapped Zazpi's wrists in strips of fabric torn from the quilted blanket. One of them smashed his face into the thin carpet, and the stench of mildew rushed up his nose.

As Zazpi fought to shake them off, Thomas's screams split the air.

"Thomas!" Amaya shouted. "Thomas, wake up!"

"Mommy?"

The pressure on Zazpi's back released, and he rolled over to find Inguma standing over him. Unlike before, Zazpi could see the god's face clearly. Leathered skin clung to bone, and Inguma's red eyes flashed. He roared with rage, rattling the television on the dresser, then pointed a long, gnarled finger at Zazpi.

"I warned you—you will pay. I cursed you with sleep, and now I give you this: your dreams shall always be dark and twisted by fear. Never shall you know true rest." The god snapped his fingers, and a shining onyx box appeared at his feet.

The lid flew open, and Zazpi's brothers marched past him to climb inside. He searched their faces with desperate eyes, looking for any sign of the imps he loved in these empty shells.

He found none.

Another snap and Inguma dissolved, taking the box with him.

Amaya fell to her knees beside Zazpi and freed him from the fabric. "Are you alright? Is it over?"

"I-I don't know," he said shakily. He struggled to process the world around him. No matter where he looked, he saw his brothers' expressionless faces as they trudged toward another prison.

"The marks on Thomas are gone. Look." Amaya picked up Zazpi and carried him to the boy, who held up his shirt proudly. No trace of the dark bruises remained.

"I'm all better," Thomas said, eyes shining. "Can I go swimming now?"

Amaya watched Thomas splash in the pool's shallow end. The motel office had gouged her on a pair of inflatable water wings and a tube of sunscreen, but it was worth the expense. She hadn't seen her son so joyful since before Glenn left.

"Zazpi!" Thomas called. "Come swim with me!"

The imp shrank back against Amaya. She had propped him against her hip, hoping a casual observer would assume he was just an oddly dressed action figure. It didn't seem to be an issue; nobody else was at the pool so early in the day.

"What do you say, Zazpi?" she asked. "Want to get in the

water?"

He wrinkled his nose. "It smells unnatural. How can Thomas stand that sharp odor?"

She laughed. "You don't have to."

Zazpi didn't reply, and she studied him for a few moments. He watched Thomas as closely as she did and hadn't left his side all morning. Over breakfast, while Thomas was absorbed in a cartoon, Zazpi had told her everything that happened the night before—the way his brothers had looked before they disappeared and the promise Inguma made that Zazpi would be greeted by nightmares whenever he slept. She hadn't seen the old god, but Zazpi's words painted a picture vivid enough to assure her it was better that way.

Her heart ached for the imp as she watched him. She wasn't sure which was worse: being afraid to fall asleep or knowing you would never see your family again. One thing couldn't help the other, and she worried for his future.

"I hope you'll choose to stay with us," she said, hoping to emphasize that she wouldn't force him.

He glanced up at her. "What would I do? Fix things?"

She shrugged. "If you want. Or you could play with Thomas, take up a hobby, be a couch potato—whatever floats your boat."

Zazpi was quiet for a long time. Amaya didn't press him.

"Could I read your books?" he asked after a while.

"Of course." She smiled, wondering if the imp had any idea what a library was.

"I think I would like that."

"You do seem to like stories." She brushed a stray piece of carpet lint from Zazpi's beret. "Maybe you could even write them."

"Write them...." His voice trailed off. When he looked at her again, tears glistened in his eyes. "About my brothers?"

A hard lump grew in Amaya's throat, and she had to clear it

before answering. "I would love to hear them."

"Yes. Stories about my brothers. Stories about my nightmares." He was nodding now, tiny hands flexed in his lap. "There is much work to do."

STORY NOTES

Author's note: I put these at the end of the book rather than before each entry so I didn't have to worry about spoilers. Reader beware.

NO SOLICITING

My favorite part of this story is Frankie, who was inspired by my great-aunt's African Grey parrot, Emilio. Despite living in Spain most of his life, he spoke English, and all his favorite words were four letters long. He oozed attitude, and I think he knew exactly how inappropriate he was being—and loved it.

I pulled a snarky bird into the story to help me balance out the rage that drove me to write it. The sound of a doorbell sends a zing of anxiety straight into my belly when it's not expected, especially in the summer. My neighborhood must have a reputation for being full of hot leads because good weather guarantees door-to-door salespeople stopping by. I bought a "No Soliciting" sign a few years ago and, well…. After reading Doris's story, you can probably guess how effective it's been.

EMPIRE OF DIRT

Ask any nurse who's ever had to deal with me: I do not like needles. (It was hard to even type that word, ugh). I hate them so much that when I listen to "Hurt" by Nine Inch Nails, I have to block out a certain line in the first verse. I love that song, though, and it really inspired me while I was drafting Tabatha's spiteful story. I love the way the original recording builds, getting stronger and more discordant before fuzzing out completely. I wanted Tabatha's deathbed generosity to follow that arc, fuzzing out into selfishness in the end.

I played with other titles like "Balancing the Scales," which I thought might help get my point across about these twins who are on a see-saw of luck with one another, but I kept coming back to that song. If it's been awhile since you heard it, find your favorite version and give it a listen.

THE FISHERMEN

This was the story that convinced me all of this was possible. It was the first short I ever wrote in response to a call for submissions, and I'm still so proud of it.

Zoe and Topher's excursion was inspired by my weekly outings with my cousins growing up. I'm blessed with a large and closely knit extended family, and my brother and I spent a lot of time running around the then-undeveloped foothills behind my grandparent's house with our cousins and youngest uncle, collecting tadpoles and making up stories about the abandoned forts in the trees. I loved and hated wandering far enough to lose sight of my grandparent's roof—the sense of freedom was exhilarating, but I worried some "drifter" (one of so many boogeymen in the '90s) might pop out of the woods and murder us. I wanted to take those feelings and inject them into a post-apocalyptic scenario, and this was the result.

THE DEVIL'S WAY OUT

I wrote this story during the last afternoon of a writing retreat at Echo Reservoir in northern Utah in 2018. That was a painful year for me, kicking off with the unexpected passing of my beloved grandmother, and I didn't get much writing done. The autumn retreat felt like a warm bath that loosened all the pent-up emotions clogging up my brain. As I sat in the cabin, looking out over the shrunken shoreline of the reservoir and thinking about going back to regular life, this poured out of me. I cried while I wrote it. I cry when I read it. It holds all my fears of growing old and losing my grasp on the order of my memories, which sit alongside my even greater fear of not getting to grow old at all and my unhealthy habit of swimming through the past instead of facing current realities. I'm glad it got to meet the world for the first time in this collection, alongside all the other fears that clog me up inside.

FAMILY TIME

My house never had a grandfather or cuckoo clock growing up, and I'm thankful for it. I can't fall asleep if there's a ticking clock nearby, and that Westminster Quarters melody makes me nervous. It just sounds so ominous, like the clock wants to make sure I'll remember exactly what time it was before the horrible thing that will define the rest of my life happens. When I was invited to write a story for an anthology called *The Witching Time of Night*, I knew it had to revolve around a haunted version of those awful clocks.

I named the main character Maeve after Maeve Binchy, one of my favorite authors. In the original version, I gave her what I thought was a very natural sounding last name: Higgins. It came to me suspiciously quickly, but I assumed it was the product of my own incredible imagination. I didn't realize what I'd done until I was listening to *Wait Wait Don't Tell Me* and they introduced their panelists, including comedian Maeve Higgins. Whoops! Turns out I usually write short stories on weekends after listening to the radio, and I'm not as clever at naming characters as I thought.

WATCHERS' WARNING

My cats have a lot of hobbies: destroying my slippers, collecting candy wrappers, barking at birds, and swiveling their heads in unison to look at the exact same spot of nothing on the wall. I remember my friend Karen asking, "Are you watching the magic?" when her cat Belladonna did the same thing, and I thought that was a much lovelier assumption than the one my brain makes when my cats are calmly watching an invisible demon scuttle down the wall behind me.

If I was ever in any *real* danger, I would at least expect them to look vaguely concerned about my impending doom. And I have complete faith that they would come to my rescue like Ripley does if some swamp thing was after me. At least until my gluttonous tabby, George, figures out how to open Fancy Feast cans. After that, I'm probably on my own.

UNTIL DEATH

"Write about your worst fear" was the prompt that sparked this flash piece. I knew it would be hard to pick just one, but in the end, I chose the fear that pierces my heart the deepest. When we were younger, my husband and I used to talk about which would be worse: going first or being left behind. We haven't brought the topic back up since our first gray hairs started coming in.

This is the shortest piece of fiction I've ever published, and I didn't think it would find a home until *The NoSleep Podcast* chose to include it in one of their "Suddenly Shocking" volumes. Thank you, Olivia!

A FRIEND IN NEED

Like most of my stories, "A Friend in Need" was born out of anxiety. Someone asked for a small favor, but circumstances prevented me from doing it. My friend didn't mind. Everything was fine. All the same, I worried about the unintended consequences of my inability to help. What if, because I wasn't there, they left their house five minutes later than they otherwise would have and got into a horrible car accident? (Thanks a lot, *Final Destination* movies.) Then, because I'm an omnidirectional agonizer, I imagined the worst thing that could've happened if I *had* helped—what if I was the one who got into an accident on my way to them? What if I ran out of gas and, while walking along the side of the road with a gas can in hand, was captured by some forgotten demonic force?

It's better those catastrophes happen on the page than in my life, so here we are.

THE BUMP

This was my love letter to my early horror addiction, *Scary Stories to Tell in the Dark*. I loved the folklore style of those stories, like every single one was something that could have happened in my own town. Working on it made me think of all the horror that was right in front of me when I was a kid, like the nursery rhymes we sang in daycare. Putting aside how inherently creepy it is to hear a group of tiny children's voices sing just about *anything*, the origins and lyrics of a lot of those songs are super dark. This one gave me a nice, healthy fear of concussions: "It's raining, it's pouring, the old man is snoring. Went to bed with a bump on his head and didn't wake up in the morning."

Yep. Totally normal, happy lyrics.

THE THING INSIDE JACKY JENSEN'S GARAGE

An assignment to write about a local cryptid sent me down the rabbit hole of Utah lore for this story. After sifting through a lot of Bear Lake Monster sightings, I came across a short mention of a furry—yet reptilian—creature skulking around the Huntsville Cemetery, not far north from some ghost hunting I'd done outside Coalville. That area has a hushed, heavy energy at night that makes wandering the darkness with a group of friends and some dowsing rods feel deliciously spooky. I love the idea that there's a monster hanging out in a cemetery up there, munching on flowers and garbage Sasquatch-style and only turning violent if pushed beyond his limits.

INGUMA WE TRUST

My dad and I often talk about our nightmares (bad as mine are, his are downright terrifying), and we have something in common: our worst nightmares come when we're sleeping on our backs. The logical side of my brain thinks it's because our bellies are exposed and our unconscious minds aren't happy about it, but the other half of my brain can't stop thinking about the illustration of Inguma by Basque artist Raquel Alzate (published in *Mitologika: Una Visión Contemporánea de Los Seres Mágicos de Euskadi* by Aritza Bergara). Seeing the god of nightmares crouching on the belly of his sleeping victim gave me chills, and I've been a little obsessed with Inguma ever since.

I wrote the first draft of this story in March 2020, just as the pandemic hit Utah. A week after I finished that draft, an earthquake hit Salt Lake City and rattled me out of bed. I was a mess for a while after that, overwhelmed by anxiety and unable to imagine what the future looked like. That bled through in subsequent rewrites pretty hard but—like I imagine it will for Zazpi—writing helped me cope.

ABOUT THE AUTHOR

Caryn Larrinaga is a Basque-American mystery, horror, and urban fantasy writer. Her debut novel, *Donn's Hill*, was awarded the League of Utah Writers 2017 Silver Quill in the adult novel category and was a 2017 Dragon Award finalist.

Watching scary movies through split fingers terrified Caryn as a child, and those nightmares inspire her to write now. Her 90-year-old house has a colorful history, and the creaking walls and narrow hallways send her running (never walking) up the stairs. Exploring her fears through writing makes Caryn feel a little less foolish for wanting a buddy to accompany her into the tool shed.

Caryn lives near Salt Lake City, Utah, with her husband and their clowder of cats. She is an active member of the Science Fiction and Fantasy Writers of America, the Horror Writers Association, the Cat Writers Association, and the League of Utah Writers.

Visit www.carynlarrinaga.com for free short fiction and true tales of haunted places.

facebook.com/carynwrites

twitter.com/carynlarrinaga

instagram.com/carynlarrinaga

amazon.com/author/carynlarrinaga

goodreads.com/carynlarrinaga

bookbub.com/authors/caryn-larrinaga

Ghosts. Psychics. Murder.
Just another day in Donn's Hill.

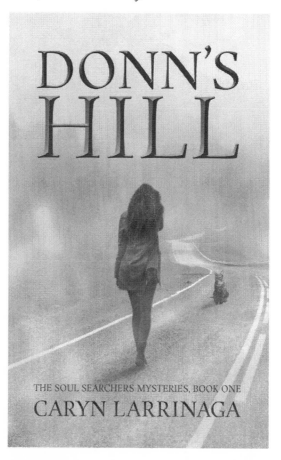

THE SOUL SEARCHERS MYSTERIES, BOOK ONE

CARYN LARRINAGA

2017 WINNER

LEAGUE
of
UTAH WRITERS
Silver Quill

"A genre-bending gem of a book,
cozy meets horror meets cat fancier
in a unique town of psychic tourism
and ghostly secrets."

*- Johnny Worthen, award winning
author of THE FINGER TRAP,
THE BRAND DEMAND and
WHAT IMMORTAL HAND*

CONTENT WARNING

The stories in this book contain content that may trigger a strong or potentially harmful emotional response in some readers, including:

Death and dying
Death of a loved one
Mental illness
Murder
Mutilation of corpses
Threatening a child